MYSTERY AT MAYPENNY'S

**Trixie
Belden**

Your TRIXIE BELDEN Library

Trixie Belden and the
MYSTERY AT MAYPENNY'S

BY KATHRYN KENNY

Cover by Ben Otero

® GOLDEN PRESS
Western Publishing Company, Inc.
Racine, Wisconsin

ISBN 0-307-21552-0

CONTENTS

MYSTERY AT MAYPENNY'S

Mr. Maypenny's Mystery • 1

"YOU'D BETTER HURRY, Trixie," Brian Belden called up the stairs. "The school bus will be here any minute."

"I'm coming!" his fourteen-year-old sister shouted from her bedroom. Hurriedly, she finished buttoning her blouse and tucked it firmly into the waistband of her pants. She hunted frantically for her hairbrush, which was buried under the piles of books and papers on her dresser. Finding it, she ran it through her sandy curls without bothering to look in the mirror.

"If Brian would help me get Bobby ready for school instead of reading the sports section of the paper, I might be ready on time once in a while," she grumbled. Then she blushed, realizing she was being unfair to her older brother. All of the Beldens had their share of chores to do. Getting Bobby, the youngest of the four Belden children, ready for school in the morning was Trixie's task. On mornings when he dawdled, Trixie had to rush. But in the afternoon, Trixie often had free time to spend with her best friend, Honey Wheeler, while Brian and Mart were busy with yard work and repairs around the house.

Trixie shoved her feet into a pair of loafers, gathered up her schoolbooks, and started out of the room. Then, remembering that the weatherman had predicted cool temperatures, she hurried back and grabbed a red jacket off its hanger in the closet. The jacket had "B.W.G." embroidered in white across the back. It was one of seven jackets Honey Wheeler had made for a semisecret club called the Bob-Whites of the Glen. The members were Trixie and her two brothers, Honey and her adoptive brother Jim Frayne, and two other friends, Dan Mangan and Di Lynch.

The club had been formed shortly after Honey and her parents had moved to the Manor House, a huge estate just down the road from the Beldens' modest Crabapple Farm. The club devoted itself to helping people who were in need, such as a group of Mexican children whose school had been destroyed by a hurricane. In addition, the Bob-Whites frequently found themselves in the midst of a mystery, thanks to Trixie and Honey, who planned to be partners in a detective agency when they finished school.

The other Bob-Whites teased Honey and Trixie about their knack for uncovering mysteries, but they all pitched in eagerly to find a solution when a new case presented itself.

As Trixie ran down the stairs on this September morning, however, the only mystery on her mind was whether the school bus had left without her. She heard the kitchen door slam and realized that Brian and Mart were already leaving. Pulling on her jacket as she went, she hurried through the kitchen after them, shouting a hurried "Good-bye, Moms" over her shoulder.

Trixie caught up with her brothers halfway down the long driveway to the road where the school bus stopped to pick them up. The bus was already visible in the distance, and they all had to run the last few feet.

They climbed breathlessly onto the bus and walked to the back where Honey, Jim, and Dan were saving seats for them. Di Lynch had taken a late vacation with her parents and would not return to Sleepyside for almost two weeks. As the bus started up, Trixie looked through the rear window and saw a battered-looking green car pulling into the driveway of Crabapple Farm. Neither the car nor the driver looked familiar, and her mother hadn't mentioned expecting a visitor. Trixie wondered briefly who it could be, then lost herself in the chatter of her friends.

"The Belden contingent came perilously close to missing their means of public transport this antemeridian," Mart Belden said. Mart was Trixie's almost-twin. He was eleven months older than his sister and had the same sandy hair and freckles. His cropped hair and love of big words were the major differences between them.

"I thought for a minute there we'd have to take the jalopy this morning," Brian agreed. He and Jim, the two oldest Bob-Whites, each had a driver's license. Brian had worked hard to save the money for the secondhand car that was his pride and joy. It was also a source of teasing from the rest of the Bob-Whites, since it took all of Brian's considerable mechanical ability to keep it running.

"I'm glad you managed to make it," Dan Mangan said. "Mr. Maypenny asked me to give everyone a message this morning."

Mr. Maypenny was the gamekeeper for the

large preserve that Mr. Wheeler had bought and stocked with deer, pheasant, ducks, and other animals. He lived in a little cabin on a pie-shaped section of land he owned in the middle of the preserve. Dan had lived there, too, ever since his uncle, Regan, the Wheelers' groom, had brought Dan to Sleepyside to get him away from the bad crowd he'd been hanging around with in New York City. Dan had been sullen and quiet when he'd first come to Sleepyside. Now he was a loyal and helpful Bob-White, although his work for Mr. Maypenny sometimes kept him away from club activities.

"What's the message?" Brian asked.

"Well," Dan said slowly, "it's like this." He paused and looked first at Honey and then at Trixie, a teasing glint in his eye. "It seems he has a mystery for us to solve."

Trixie and Honey both gasped at once, and Mart put both his hands to his head as if to protect himself from an avalanche. "Speak no more," he said in mock despair. "I can say with certitude that you have already unleashed a tempest in my sleuth sibling and her loyal confederate."

"If you mean that Honey and I are excited at being asked to solve a mystery, Mart, you're absolutely right," Trixie said. "Usually grown-ups

17

are busy trying to keep us *out* of mysteries." She turned her attention from her brother back to Dan Mangan. "What is it?" she asked eagerly. "Poachers? Or did Mr. Maypenny discover a hiding place for stolen property on the preserve? What?"

Dan shook his head ruefully. "I should have known my little joke would backfire," he said. "I've got you much too worked up. It's really nothing exciting, I'm afraid. Mr. Maypenny wants us to help him find a tree after school this afternoon. That's all."

Honey's huge hazel eyes showed her confusion as she looked from Dan to Trixie and back again.

Trixie, too, looked confused—but only for a moment. Then her temper flared. "There are thousands of trees in those woods, Dan Mangan," she said. "Why would Mr. Maypenny need our help to find a tree? You're just teasing us. I bet it is a poacher, after all."

But when Trixie presented her theory to Mr. Maypenny that afternoon, the wiry old man shook his head. "I almost wish it were a poacher, Trixie," he said. "It would be a lot less embarrassing to admit I had a poacher on the place than to admit I forgot where that tree is. But forget I did. You see, I noticed a tree along the edge of the path between here and Lytell's store.

It's badly rotted at the base. If I cut it down now, I can make sure it falls away from the path. Otherwise, this being storm season, a big wind will come along, and, sure as I'm standing here, that tree will fall across the path." He shrugged his broad, slightly stooped shoulders. "I should have marked it right away, but I thought I'd remember where it was. Well, I didn't. So I decided to have Dan ask for your help instead of keeping my stupidity to myself."

"We're glad to help, Mr. Maypenny," Honey said tactfully. "Why don't you show us the general area where you saw the tree so we can start looking for it?"

Trixie looked at Honey appreciatively. Her friend was always so considerate of other people's feelings. Trixie, too, had sensed Mr. Maypenny's embarrassment at having to admit his mistake, but it was Honey who had rescued him by suggesting they begin the search.

The tall, gaunt old man led the Bob-Whites down the path and pointed out the general location of the tree. They spread out and began their search.

Predictably, it was Jim, the best woodsman among the Bob-Whites, who found the tree. The others heard his triumphant whoop and headed toward it.

19

"That's it," Mr. Maypenny said, after he quickly examined the base of the tree Jim pointed out.

"Let's get to work," Jim said, picking up the ax he'd carried with him. After he'd taken out a V-shaped section of the side away from the path, Dan and Brian stepped in with a saw. Soon the tree toppled harmlessly into the woods.

Mr. Maypenny smiled and shoved his red cap to the back of his head. "Hunter's stew today, if you folks are interested," he said. "I've had a batch simmering since this morning, just in case you young 'uns worked up an appetite out here in the woods."

"Yummy-yum!" Trixie shouted. "Mr. Maypenny's hunter's stew is just about my favorite thing in the whole world! Let's eat!"

But Brian, the most level-headed of the Bob-Whites, shook his head. "I'm sorry, Mr. Maypenny. I love your hunter's stew as much as Trixie does. But it's pretty close to dinner time. We have to be going home."

Mr. Maypenny nodded. "I figured it might be close to dinner time when you'd finished up here. That's why I went ahead and called your folks this afternoon to ask if you could stay for dinner. I must say," he continued, a smile smoothing out the lines at the corners of his mouth, "nobody seemed very disappointed that you wouldn't be around to eat them out of house and home tonight. So I guess it's my hunter's stew or go hungry."

"Well, then," Mart said, "shall we commence with the comestibles?"

"I have a better idea," Trixie said. "Let's eat!"

Laughing, the Bob-Whites trooped into Mr. Maypenny's cottage.

Later, as the Bob-Whites were savoring the rich combination of fresh vegetables and tasty venison simmered for hours in a thick, dark broth, Brian said, "I wish you'd ask for favors more often, Mr. Maypenny. You have such a terrific way of repaying them!"

The other Bob-Whites smiled in agreement, but Mr. Maypenny frowned. "You're welcome to come over for stew any time you like, Brian. You know that. But I hope I don't have to ask for any more favors. I've been an independent old cuss all my life, and it rankles me to ask for help. I wouldn't have had to this time if that young whippersnapper Matt Wheeler hadn't got me all riled up."

"D-Daddy?" Honey's voice came out as a squeak. Her friends looked at one another nervously. Mr. Maypenny had had his share of disagreements with the big, redheaded Matthew

Wheeler in the past, starting when the wealthy businessman had tried to buy the independent older man's little section of land for his game preserve. Mr. Maypenny had refused even the highest offers, and Mr. Wheeler had finally had to admit that his money couldn't buy everything. The two had eventually reached a truce: Mr. Maypenny kept his land and took over as the gamekeeper that Mr. Wheeler sorely needed. But the Bob-Whites all knew that neither man had lost his stubborn streak. If Mr. Maypenny was "riled up," it could mean trouble.

"Are you and Dad having problems, Mr. Maypenny?" Jim asked. His tone was casual, but his face looked grim under its shock of red hair. Jim's loyalty to his adoptive father was intense.

Mr. Maypenny suddenly looked embarrassed.

"I'm sorry, Jim," he said sincerely. "I plain forgot that Matt Wheeler was your father. You kids are so nice and reasonable that it just doesn't seem possible."

Trixie had to bite her lower lip to keep from giggling at Mr. Maypenny's backhanded compliment to Honey and Jim.

There was a smile playing around Jim's mouth, too, as he asked, "What's Dad being un-nice and unreasonable about?"

Mr. Maypenny shook his head, as if he

couldn't believe what he was about to say. "Matt Wheeler came over here a couple of days ago just as I was getting ready to go down to Lytell's store. Wheeler had some big shot from International Pine along with him."

"International Pine?" Brian interrupted. "You mean the same company that drained the swamp to build that new furniture factory a while back?"

Mr. Maypenny nodded. "The same," he said. "It seems that after they drained the swamp, killing all those rare plants and driving the animals out of their homes, and after they built their big factory that belches smoke out all over the place, they started doing pretty well for themselves. So well, in fact, that now they want to expand. They went to Matt Wheeler and made him an offer on a parcel of land. Some of the land in that parcel is his, and some is mine. Matt Wheeler said *he'd* be happy to sell, and he came over here to try to talk me into doing the same."

Mr. Maypenny paused and shook his head again as he recalled the conversation. The Bob-Whites sat in shocked silence as he continued. "Of course, as soon as I realized what they were talking about, I told them my answer was no and that was as final as final could be. Matt got all red in the face and asked me to listen to him talk some more of his nonsense. He even hinted that he might go right ahead and sell his land and leave me with a factory on my doorstep and no money to show for my trouble. That's what was on my mind when I noticed that tree, and that's why I couldn't remember where I'd seen it," he concluded.

The Bob-Whites' shocked silence continued for several moments after Mr. Maypenny stopped talking. The game preserve was Mr. Wheeler's pride and joy, they knew. None of them could imagine that he would even consider selling part of it—especially not to a company that planned to build a factory on the land, driving the animals out of their homes.

Jim finally broke the silence. "I don't believe it!" he said angrily.

"What Jim means is, there must be some logical explanation for what Daddy did," Honey said. The expression on her face was a deeply troubled one, but, as always, her first concern was preventing an argument.

Mr. Maypenny, however, was not afraid of an argument. "There's an explanation, all right," he said firmly. "That International Pine fellow offered your dad a pile of money for that land, that's all. I can understand your wanting to stick up for him. There's no doubt but what Matt

Wheeler is a good father. But he was a shrewd businessman first—and last, and always. He's not going to pass up a chance to make good money when it's handed to him on a platter."

"You're wrong!" Jim rose to his feet, his voice just barely below a shout. "Dad has plenty of money, and plenty of ways to make more without destroying wildlife. He wouldn't sell the preserve or any piece of it to a company like International Pine. There's some explanation for what happened here the other day, and I'm going to find out what it is." Without another word, Jim walked out the front door.

Once again, a shocked silence reigned in the cottage. Honey's hazel eyes were brimming with tears, and she lowered her head so that her honey-colored hair hid her face.

After a moment, Mr. Maypenny's angry mood gave way to an apologetic one, and he walked around the table to put a gnarled hand on Honey's shoulder. "Don't fret because of what I said," he told the girl. "I don't think your dad is right about wanting to sell to International Pine, but that doesn't mean I think he's a bad person. Maybe there is some other explanation. If there is, your brother will soon find out about it. When Matt Wheeler adopted Jim Frayne, he got more than a head of red hair to match his own. He got a temper just as fiery and a stubborn streak just as wide."

Honey raised her head, revealing the beginnings of a smile on her tear-stained face. "You're right, Mr. Maypenny," she said. "Jim will get Daddy to tell him what the problem is. And I'll bet it will be a reason even you would have accepted if you'd let him tell you about it the other day."

Mr. Maypenny threw back his head and laughed. "What you're saying, Honey Wheeler, is that your dad and brother aren't the only stubborn ones around these parts. And you're right. I should have listened to your father's explanation. It might have saved me some embarrassment— and a whole batch of hunter's stew!"

The Bob-Whites laughed, feeling relieved that the tension had been broken—and a little self-conscious as they realized that the enormous pot of stew Mr. Maypenny had set before them was now almost empty.

Suddenly Dan Mangan snapped his fingers and jumped to his feet. "You're not the only forgetful person around these parts, either, Mr. Maypenny," he said. "I picked up a letter for you down at the mailbox, and I completely forgot to give it to you." He left the room for a moment to retrieve the letter from his jacket and came back holding out a long white envelope.

Mr. Maypenny regarded the envelope curiously for a moment before he took it from Dan's hand. The old man had lived his entire life on this small piece of land. Letters from the outside world were a rarity. He seldom even thought to check his mailbox, which was almost a quarter of a mile away, on the road to town.

Finally he took the envelope and held it in his gnarled hands. He looked at the return address and postmark for a clue as to the sender. Finding none, he took out the letter and began to read.

The room was uncomfortably quiet again as the Bob-Whites tried not to break his concentration by either staring at him or talking among themselves.

Mr. Maypenny suddenly folded the letter and rose abruptly from his chair, clearing his throat. "Excuse me," he said. "I'll be right back. I—" He broke off, turned, and left the room—but not before Trixie saw the glint of tears in the old man's eyes.

A Clash of Viewpoints · 2

TRIXIE AND THE OTHERS stared after him in concern. "Do you think he's all right?" Trixie asked softly. "I hope the letter wasn't bad news."

As she spoke, Mr. Maypenny returned to the room as abruptly as he had left it. He was wiping his eyes with a handkerchief, but there was a broad grin on his face. "It isn't bad news at all, Trixie," he said. "In fact, it's about the best news I've had in ages."

"Who's the letter from, Mr. Maypenny?" Trixie asked curiously.

"It's from my nephew, David Maypenny," the gamekeeper said, sitting back down at the table.

He unfolded the letter again and stared down at it as if he couldn't quite believe it was real.

"You never told me you had a nephew," Dan Mangan said.

"I'd almost forgotten I did have one," the old man said. "I've never even met the boy. Actually, he's not a boy anymore. He must be almost thirty by now." Mr. Maypenny's face clouded over, and his eyes glistened. "I quarreled with the boy's father, my late brother, several years before David was born. My brother moved to the city and I never saw him again. I later heard that he'd married and had a son. Then I heard he'd died. I—I wrote to the boy's mother then, asking if I could do anything, send a bit of money from time to time to help out." He sighed. "I never got an answer to my letter. I figured my brother had turned her against me—turned the boy against me, too, probably. I never wrote again."

"And now your nephew has written to you," Trixie said softly. "But why, after all these years?"

Mr. Maypenny shrugged. "I don't know, exactly. He just says he thinks it's time we buried the hatchet and got to know one another. He has some vacation time coming, and he wants to come up here for a visit."

"That's wonderful!" Honey said. Her own

unhappiness was completely forgotten in the face of Mr. Maypenny's good news. "When is he going to come?"

"He says he'd like to drive up the end of next week. He says he won't come unless he hears from me, though," Mr. Maypenny said. "I think I'll write to him tonight."

Brian rose from the table and stretched. "I think that sounds like a good idea, Mr. Maypenny. And I think it would be a good idea if we went home and let you get started with your letter. It's getting late."

"A perspicuous observation," Mart said, rising to his feet. "I have an arduous assignment in geometry still ahead of me this evening, and I seem to recall that dear Beatrix also transported a textbook or two from the halls of academe."

Trixie wrinkled her nose at the sound of her hated full name, which Mart used only when he wanted to tease her. Then she too stood up. "I do have some homework to do yet tonight. Thanks for the great stew, Mr. Maypenny. And we'll look forward to meeting your nephew."

Honey was also ready to leave. "Thank you for the dinner, Mr. Maypenny," she said.

"Thank you for your help," Mr. Maypenny said. "Tell Jim I said thanks, too. And—and tell him I'm sorry for getting him all upset tonight. I hope he won't stay mad at me."

"He won't," Honey replied. "Jim's anger is pretty powerful, but it usually doesn't last very long."

Calling out final good-nights, the Bob-Whites walked out into the deepening twilight. The Beldens walked Honey down the path to the Manor House until they could see the front door. They waited until their friend was safely inside before they turned and walked back to their own house.

Trixie pulled her red Bob-White jacket close to her body to ward off the evening chill. "It's beginning to feel like fall," she said. "I just hope this cool air wakes me up before we get home. It's been a long day, and I still have to read ten pages in my history book before I go to bed."

"It really isn't that late," Brian said. "It's only a little after seven o'clock. So much has happened, it feels as if it should be midnight."

Trixie nodded. "We haven't even been home since we left for school this morning. Oh, that reminds me! There was a car pulling into our driveway this morning just as we left on the bus. I was going to ask Moms about it this afternoon, but I never did, of course. I'll have to do that as soon as we get home."

But when Trixie and her brothers walked

through the kitchen door, the sound of Bobby's screams drove all other thoughts from their minds.

"I *won't* go to bed," they heard him wail. "I hurried an' hurried to get ready for school this morning 'cause Trixie said she'd read me a story before I went to bed tonight, if I hurried. She promised!"

Trixie groaned while Mart chuckled and Brian shook his head sympathetically. "It sounds as if you 'forgotted' something in the excitement over at Mr. Maypenny's," Brian said.

Trixie nodded, wrinkling her freckled nose. "But Bobby remembered, as usual. There's no escaping it, I guess."

Just then Bobby spotted Trixie. His wails stopped immediately, and he ran to her. "Come on, Trixie. Come and read me a story," he demanded.

"All right," Trixie said. "You go crawl into bed while I drop off my books in my room. I'll be right there."

By the time she was halfway through the story, the little boy's eyelids were drooping. When she finished and closed the book, he was sound asleep. She stood up and tiptoed out of his room, pausing to look back at his peacefully sleeping figure as she turned out the light.

Walking down the hallway to her own room,

she muttered, "I wish someone would read me ten pages of history while *I'm* drifting off to sleep." In her room, she picked up the book and flopped down on the bed. She discovered when she started reading that the chapter she had been assigned was about the Battle of Saratoga, the turning point in the Revolutionary War. She read on with a growing feeling of excitement.

Saratoga was more than just a history lesson to Trixie. She and Honey had visited the town together when Regan had disappeared from the Wheeler estate. They had tracked the groom to Saratoga and persuaded him to come back to Sleepyside. They had also solved a crime committed years before and prevented another one in the process.

During the trip, Trixie had been impressed by Honey's knowledge of the history of Saratoga. Now she found that what Honey had told her then was true, and being able to picture in her mind the areas that were being described in the book made the reading easier. The dates and facts all fell into place in one reading, and the story of the battle was actually exciting.

When Trixie finished the chapter and closed the book, she felt as if only a few minutes had passed. She was startled to discover that the time, according to her alarm clock, was eight-thirty. Almost an hour had gone by!

She was startled, too, to hear voices drifting up from downstairs. The Beldens were an early-rising family. Usually by this time the house was quiet, with Bobby asleep for the night and the three older children in their rooms doing homework or getting ready for bed.

Trixie stood up, stretched, and walked out of her room and down the stairs.

"So you see," her father was saying as she reached the living room, "Matt Wheeler does have his reasons."

"Reasons for what?" Trixie demanded.

"For selling land to International Pine," Brian told her. His voice was soft, but the expression on his face was grim. "We were just telling Dad about our visit with Mr. Maypenny."

."And I was telling your brothers why Matt Wheeler is considering selling some land for the factory expansion," Mr. Belden added.

"Then there is an explanation, after all, just as Jim said there was!" Trixie exclaimed. She perched on the edge of the couch where her father was sitting. "What's going on?" she asked excitedly.

Peter Belden smiled at his daughter. "There's nothing mysterious about it, if that's what you're hoping," he warned. "There are some details I can't reveal, however." Mr. Belden worked at the bank in Sleepyside. His job gave him access to a lot of confidential information, which he was very careful never to talk about at home. "I can give you just the basic details, which I have already told your brothers. When International Pine first announced that they had bought that swampland along the river and intended to drain the swamp and build a furniture factory, some people in this area were upset."

"I was one of those people," Brian said. "That swamp had lots of wild plants and herbs that can't be found anywhere else around here." Brian intended to become a doctor, and he had been interested in the plants that the early settlers in the area had used to cure diseases in the days before doctors and drugstores.

Peter Belden nodded. "Exactly," he said. "I was not one of the people who opposed International Pine. The fact is that there's a desperate need for jobs in this area. The days of the small family farm are gone. So, for the most part, are the days of the small storekeeper. With the prices of land and equipment rising every year, they can't compete with the larger operations."

"What about Mr. Lytell?" Trixie demanded. "His little store seems to do all right." The tiny, old-fashioned store along Glen Road was a frequent stop for the Bob-Whites, in spite of the fact that the store's owner was not always friendly to the young people.

Mr. Belden shook his head. "Think about what you buy at Mr. Lytell's, Trixie. Your mother sends you for a loaf of bread or a carton of milk, or you stop in for a can of soda when you're out riding. That isn't much, compared to the amount we spend at the supermarket in Sleepyside, where we do most of our shopping.

"The fact is, Mr. Lytell could do twice as well by selling his store and going to work as the manager of a larger store in town."

"Then why doesn't he?" Trixie asked.

"He simply doesn't want to. To Mr. Lytell, money isn't as important as being his own boss and living in the area where he grew up. That's the choice he's made."

"Not many people would make that choice," Brian observed.

"Someone with a growing family to support would be almost sure to choose the higher salary," Mr. Belden agreed. "Then the choice is a long commute to work or moving the entire family out of Sleepyside."

"Aren't there any jobs in Sleepyside?" Trixie asked.

"There are a few," her father replied. "But most of the jobs in a small town are in what are called service occupations, like banking or teaching. They depend on serving people in manufacturing or farming occupations. In this area, which has never had much manufacturing and is seeing less and less farming, the number of jobs in service occupations is declining, too.

"That's why a factory like International Pine is a twofold blessing in an area like Sleepyside. They employ people directly in their factory. And, because their workers need groceries and haircuts and savings accounts and so forth, they create jobs indirectly, too."

"Matt Wheeler knows that," Brian told Trixie. "That's why he considered selling some of the preserve for the factory expansion."

"It sounds as though Jim was right," Trixie said. "If Mr. Maypenny had waited to hear Mr. Wheeler's explanation, he would have gone along with the plan to sell the land."

"I'm afraid not, Trixie," Mrs. Belden said. "There are some people to whom saving the land is the most important consideration of all. They would say that people who want high-paying jobs have to pay the price by moving to the city."

"I can see how Mr. Maypenny would feel that way," Trixie said. "He's been living off the land all his life."

"It isn't just Mr. Maypenny who feels that

way," her mother told her. "I had a visitor this morning who opposes the expansion just as strongly as Mr. Maypenny does."

"The man in the green car!" Trixie exclaimed. "I've been wondering about him since this morning. Who was he? What did he want?"

Mrs. Belden smiled. "I should have known my eagle-eyed daughter would have spotted the car. The young man's name was John Score. He represents a group called CAUSE—Citizens Alarmed and United to Save the Ecology. His group has heard about the proposed expansion, and they're trying to stop it."

"Stop it?" Trixie echoed. "How can they do that? If International Pine finds someone who's willing to sell them the land, then they can build on it, can't they?"

"Not necessarily," Mr. Belden said. "For one thing, there are zoning regulations that restrict the ways in which land can be used. Some places are zoned only for private homes, for example. Others are zoned only for farming.

"And even if International Pine finds a piece of land that is properly zoned for their uses, there's still the matter of public opinion. That's where a group like CAUSE comes in."

"John Score is trying to get people around here to sign a petition against the expansion," Mrs.

Belden said. "If he can get enough signatures, it will prove that people don't want the factory to expand. That would make it very hard for someone to sell to the company—if they want their neighbors to keep speaking to them."

"Oh, woe," Trixie moaned, covering her face with her hands. "When you said there was an explanation for Mr. Wheeler's offering to sell part of the preserve to International Pine, I thought you meant a *simple* explanation. This is the most complicated thing I've ever heard of."

"Our sophisticated elucidation is causing mental torment for our simpleminded sibling," Mart said. "Allow me to summarize. Point one: People need jobs. Point two: Animals and plants need land. Point three: These two needs are sometimes mutually exclusive. Point four: It's a very emotional issue. Point five: There are going to be a lot more quarrels before this issue is settled."

"I'd say that's a very accurate summary," Mr. Belden said. "You've already heard of an argument between Mr. Wheeler and Mr. Maypenny, and you've seen one between Mr. Maypenny and Jim—and the proposed expansion isn't even common knowledge yet."

"It will be soon," Mrs. Belden said. "John Score is devoting all his time to circulating those petitions. It won't be long before everyone in the area is taking sides on the issue."

"Which side did you take, Moms?" Trixie asked. "Did you sign the petition or not?"

"I didn't sign the petition," Mrs. Belden said. "But that doesn't mean I've taken a side. It's just the opposite, in fact. I can see both sides of this issue a little too clearly to make up my mind one way or the other."

Trixie turned to her brothers. "What about you two? Which side are you taking?"

Her brothers looked at each other, each wanting the other to speak first. Finally Brian broke the silence. "I don't know, either, Trix," he said. "I love that preserve, and I'd hate to see it changed. But I'd hate to see a whole way of life ruined, too. And that's what will happen if the economy in Sleepyside goes bad. The small-town way of life will disappear. I need more time—and more facts—before I make up my mind."

"Brian said it all," Mart said simply, too lost in thought to come up with his usual string of big words. "I only hope the issue can be settled without destroying too many friendships."

Thinking about the anger she'd seen on Jim's face as he left Mr. Maypenny's cottage, Trixie silently agreed.

"One thing I do know," Mr. Belden said. "We can't settle this issue here tonight. I suggest we

all get some sleep. We'll have plenty of op-
portunity to make up our minds about International Pine's expansion in weeks to come. In fact,
I doubt that the people of Sleepyside will talk
about anything else until the matter is settled."

Trixie and her brothers said good night to their
parents and trooped up the stairs to their rooms.

Once she was settled in her bed, Trixie felt
herself quickly drifting off to sleep. But her mind
was still a confused jumble of thoughts about
Mr. Maypenny, Mr. Wheeler, Jim, and a lot of
other people she didn't know but whose lives
were bound to be affected, one way or the other,
by the furniture factory's proposed expansion.
"I'm glad I don't have to make the final decision," she murmured as she fell asleep.

Bob-Whites Divided! · 3

THE NEXT MORNING, when Trixie climbed onto
the school bus ahead of her brothers, she scanned
the crowd of people, as usual, for Honey, Jim,
and Dan. Usually there was a frantic wave from
one of the three to let the Beldens know where
they were sitting. Today there was none.

For a moment, Trixie thought her friends must
have missed the bus. Then she spotted Honey sitting toward the back of the bus, staring out the
window. Dan was sitting next to her, looking at a
book that was perched on his crossed leg. There
was no sign of Jim.

Trixie felt her stomach tighten. Something was

obviously wrong. She paused, wondering what it could be. Then Brian, standing behind her, nudged her gently. "Let's go, Trix," he said. The concerned tone of his voice told her that he too had noticed something wrong.

Trixie and Brian dropped into the seat in front of Honey and Dan, and Mart took one across the aisle. For the first time, Honey turned from the window, and Trixie saw that her eyes were swollen and red-rimmed.

"What's happened, Honey?" Trixie asked. The voice that came from her tightened throat was little more than a whisper.

"Jim and Daddy had the most horrible fight this morning," Honey said, her voice shaking.

"Was it about your father's wanting to sell part of the preserve?" Brian guessed.

Honey nodded. "Mother and Daddy were out last night. They didn't get home until late, so Jim didn't get a chance to talk to them. This morning at breakfast, Jim brought the subject up. He said Mr. Maypenny had told us that International Pine wanted to expand and that Daddy was willing to go along with it. He said he wanted to know why.

"Daddy got upset right away. He called Mr. Maypenny an old fool who couldn't see past his nose. That made Jim angry, and he said he thought it was pretty shortsighted to destroy a natural wilderness that could be enjoyed by generations to come."

Trixie cringed. "Gleeps, Honey. Jim wasn't holding anything back," she said. "I bet it didn't make your father any less angry."

Honey shook her head, her eyes brimming with tears once again. "Daddy got just furious when Jim said that. He said that Jim needed to be shown a thing or two."

"Shown what?" Brian asked.

Honey shrugged helplessly. "I don't know. After Daddy said that, he turned to me and said, 'You'd better get to the bus stop. Jim won't be going to school with you this morning.' He looked so angry, I didn't dare ask any questions. I—I just left."

Trixie looked from Mart to Brian, seeking an explanation for what had happened. They said nothing. They looked as bewildered as she felt.

Surely Mr. Wheeler isn't planning to send Jim away just because Jim talked back to him, she thought, a panicky feeling pushing at her chest. When Trixie and Honey had first met Jim, he was a homeless runaway hiding from his cruel stepfather. It had taken the girls a long time to get him to trust them, and even longer to convince him that there were some grown-ups he could trust, too. The result of that trust had been a real home with the Wheelers, and his first close friendships with the other Bob-Whites. If this disagreement with his adoptive father destroyed that trust, it could destroy the home and the friendships as well.

Trixie felt tears springing into her own eyes as she imagined Jim running away again. Although she denied it to the others, and even to herself, Jim was more than a friend to Trixie. He was someone very, very special.

Brian cleared his throat. "Let's not get ourselves worked up over this thing until we find out what's really going on," he said. "Jim and Mr. Wheeler are both strong-willed and hot-tempered, but they're also devoted to each other. I don't think anything will stand between them for very long."

"Oh, Brian, you're right, of course," Trixie said gratefully. "We're silly to be so upset." She turned to her best friend. "Honey, you and I think it's horrible that Jim and your father exchanged a few words, because we're scared of yelling at someone—or of being yelled at. They aren't like we are. They'll get everything talked out, and they'll wind up respecting one another even more because of it."

"I agree with what Trixie says," Dan added.

Dan had been so quiet that the others were startled now when he finally spoke up. "Sometimes being told off hurts a lot less than not being told at all."

Honey, always alert to other people's feelings, caught the bitter edge in Dan's voice. "You're talking about yourself, aren't you, Dan?" she asked softly.

Dan nodded reluctantly. "You're right, I guess. I am talking about myself—and Mr. Maypenny. We live under the same roof and see each other every day, but he never told me about his nephew or about that visit from Mr. Wheeler that got him so upset. It hurts me that he didn't want to tell me about it."

"I'm sure he was only trying to keep you from worrying, Dan," Honey said.

"But that preserve is my home, too," Dan protested. "If someone is doing something to threaten it, I have a right to know about it."

"He turned Daddy down flat, after all," Honey pointed out. "In his mind, he probably felt there was nothing left to say."

"Besides," Brian added, "Mr. Maypenny lived alone for a long time before you came. He's not used to having anyone to share his problems with. If he said nothing about Mr. Wheeler's visit, I'm sure it was because of habit, not because of any lack of feeling for you."

Dan's only response was a shrug, a sign that he understood the logic of his friends' arguments but didn't feel entirely comforted by them.

Just then the bus pulled up in front of the school, and the Bob-Whites clambered off and walked into Sleepyside Junior-Senior High School. The friends parted inside the door to hurry to their lockers and then on to their first classes.

First it was Mr. Maypenny and Mr. Wheeler. Then it was Mr. Maypenny and Jim. Now it's Jim and Mr. Wheeler, plus Dan and Mr. Maypenny. All of them are having problems because of International Pine. Who'll be next? Trixie wondered to herself.

She soon found out. That noon, the three Beldens, Honey, and Dan assembled at their usual table in the cafeteria. They were just beginning to eat when they heard a familiar voice say, "May I join you?"

"Jim!" Trixie exclaimed, looking joyously at her redheaded friend.

Honey looked as though she wanted to throw her arms around her brother, even though it would embarrass him no end.

Brian, Mart, and Dan looked just as relieved as the girls did, and Jim started to laugh. "You'd

47

think I'd dropped out of sight for a week instead of just missing one morning of school," he said teasingly.

"I told the others about your argument with Daddy this morning," Honey confessed. "We didn't know what might have happened after I left."

Jim's face turned serious. "Dad said he was going to show me a thing or two, and that's exactly what he did. I learned more this morning than I could in ten years of school."

"What did you learn about?" Trixie asked.

"You could call it 'applied economics,' I guess," Jim said, "with some political science and even a little philosophy thrown in.

"Basically, Dad showed me how he'd come to his decision to consider the offer from International Pine. It wasn't a spur-of-the-moment thing, believe me. He has reams of information about it." Jim looked around the table. "Did you know that the population of Sleepyside has been declining at the rate of two percent per year for the past ten years?" he asked.

The other Bob-Whites shook their heads.

"Well, it has," Jim said. "At the same time, the number of jobs has decreased five percent. That means the number of people on welfare is up."

"What does all this mean, Jim?" Honey asked.

"It means a lot," Trixie said. "We talked about this with our parents last night. Sleepyside needs the jobs that the International Pine expansion can provide."

"That's it, in a nutshell," Jim said.

"So now you agree with your father about letting International Pine have the land. Is that the rest of it?" Dan asked.

"It isn't very much land—only about ten acres. Only three of those acres are Mr. Maypenny's," Jim pointed out. "Dad explained that to me, too. The ten acres they want have the best stand of virgin timber anywhere around. They'd be getting valuable raw materials along with expansion area. That's the only way they can afford to expand right now. The animals would still have hundreds of acres left, and Sleepyside would have hundreds of new jobs."

"That seems like a good solution for everyone," Honey said hopefully, looking from Jim to Dan.

Dan shook his head. "You can say that because you won't be living right under the new factory's smokestacks. Mr. Maypenny and I will. And what if the factory decides to expand again? Will another ten acres seem like a good solution someday? And then another ten, and another, until there's no game preserve left?"

"Dad won't let that happen," Jim said firmly.

"How can you be so sure?" Dan asked. "Yesterday you were shocked when you heard he wanted to sell that first ten acres; today you're behind him all the way. Maybe he'll give you the same snow job next time."

"Dan—" Honey's voice was pleading, and she put a restraining hand on the boy's arm.

"I'm sorry," Dan said. "I just—" He broke off in mid sentence, the look in his eyes begging his friends to understand.

"I can see your point of view," Jim said quietly. "But I can see my father's—Sleepyside's—too. I have to back him in selling the land."

"And I have to back Mr. Maypenny in trying to stop him," Dan replied.

The two boys looked at each other steadily for a long moment. Then Dan abruptly gathered up his things and walked away.

Trixie watched him leave. *Now the factory expansion is dividing the Bob-Whites*, she thought. She looked around at her circle of friends and found them all looking uneasily at one another. She knew that they were all echoing her own troubled thoughts: *Who's next?*

Dan's Surprise • 4

DURING THE FOLLOWING week, the news about International Pine's offer spread throughout Sleepyside. And wherever the news spread, it touched off the same arguments that had already begun among the Bob-Whites.

To many of Sleepyside's worried businessmen, who had seen their sales fall off because of rising unemployment, the possibility that International Pine might expand, creating new jobs and bringing new money into the community, seemed like a dream come true.

But to many of the older people in town, who had grown up in a Sleepyside that was quiet and rural, the expansion was more like a nightmare. They worried not only about the increase in pollution that the expansion might cause, but also about the change in their community. If their sons and grandsons left farming and shopkeeping behind to work in a factory, would they leave the old customs and traditions behind, too?

To Trixie, it began to seem as though talking about International Pine was as much a part of everyday life as eating and sleeping. Interviews with the company president and with environmental experts filled the front page of the Sleepyside *Sun*. The paper received so many letters to the editor on the expansion issue that it had to devote a full page, instead of the usual half page, to them each day.

Many of the store owners in town hung signs in their windows, either in support of or against the factory expansion.

Even in school, as she walked down the hallways, Trixie could hear her classmates arguing about the issue. In class, too, the expansion was worked into history, social studies, and science classes.

It seemed to Trixie that the only place in town where the International Pine controversy was not discussed was at the Bob-Whites' lunch table at school and in their section of the school bus.

After the argument between Jim and Dan, the Bob-Whites had agreed not to discuss International Pine, the proposed expansion, Mr. Wheeler's decision to sell, or Mr. Maypenny's decision not to. In the end, they had realized, their own opinions would have very little effect on what happened. It would be better to keep those opinions to themselves so that, whatever the outcome, the Bob-Whites would still be friends when the controversy was over.

Trixie did talk things over with her brothers when they were away from the other Bob-Whites, but she found that they continued to be as confused about the issue as she was. Because of the things their father had told them, they realized that more jobs were necessary; on the other hand, they all loved the preserve. They loved Mr. Maypenny, too. It was impossible for any of them to take a firm stand one way or the other.

On Thursday, Brian announced at the dinner table that his social studies class was going to have a debate the following week.

"The subject is International Pine, of course," he said. "I'm on the affirmative team. Dad, would you help me put together some facts and figures?"

"I will," Peter Belden said.

53

"What made you finally decide you're for the expansion?" Trixie asked.

"I haven't decided that at all, Trix," Brian said. "I'm as much on the fence as ever."

"But you're arguing for it in the debate," Trixie reminded him. "Does that mean you're for it but you're not for it? I don't understand."

Brian shrugged. "It's really not that confusing, Trix. I think this debate is important. It's the first time that the arguments for and against the expansion will really be laid out, side by side, so that people can listen to them clearly if they care to. When my social studies teacher asked for volunteers for the debate, the first two people who spoke up asked to take the negative side, opposing the expansion. They're both smart kids, and I know they'll do a good job.

"That's when I decided to take the affirmative side. I figured that with the information I can get from Dad, I can present some pretty convincing arguments. It will be an even debate. That's all I'm concerned about."

"Methinks it will take perseverance to persuade Dan Mangan of the perspicuity of the positive position," Mart said.

"Dan's in my social studies class," Brian reminded his brother. "He looked pretty tense when I volunteered. But I caught up with him after class and explained it to him. I think he understands that it's a sense of fair play that got me into this, not my personal opinion about the expansion. He can respect that, just as he can respect Jim's need to stand by his father." Brian paused and sighed. Then he added, "Still, I don't think his respect for our positions makes him feel any less lonely right now, or any less worried about whether he's going to have a place to live when the controversy is over."

"I think this whole thing has been harder on Dan than anybody else," Trixie agreed. "He's spent so much of his life trying to find a place where he feels that he belongs. He even got involved with that bad bunch in New York City—when he's not a bad person at all—just because they seemed to take an interest in him."

Brian nodded. "When Regan finally brought him to Sleepyside, Dan found a great place to live with Mr. Maypenny. He also found a group of friends, the Bob-Whites, who like him for what he is without trying to force him to be rowdy or get into trouble."

"And now his abode is in jeopardy and his companions seem alienated," Mart concluded.

"Poor Dan," Trixie said. "I think we should be extra careful to let him know he's our friend, until this whole thing is over."

"I don't think we ought to do that, Trix," Brian said. "Dan is pretty good at noticing things. Being extra nice, for whatever reason, still boils down to treating Dan differently than we have in the past. It might make him even more nervous than he already is."

Trixie wrinkled her nose, annoyed at her own stupidity. "You're right, Brian. We Bob-Whites are always teasing one another and pretending to fight. If all of a sudden we start being nice as pie to Dan, he'll probably feel like an outsider again. I guess all we can do is try to keep things as much as possible the way they've always been. But it's hard."

"Indubitably," Mart agreed gloomily.

Trixie helped her mother clear the table and wash the dishes, too busy thinking about Dan and Mr. Maypenny and Brian and Jim to do her usual chattering as she worked.

When she was finished, she laid the dish towel on the counter absentmindedly and wandered out of the kitchen. From the living room, she could hear the murmur of voices, first her father's and then Brian's, as they talked about the debate. Occasionally Mart's voice would come in briefly, too. Trixie smiled to herself. Nobody loved to argue as much as Mart did. She could imagine him pouncing on anything his father and brother said that sounded weak, tearing it apart the way the opposition would at the debate. This was one time when Brian would be grateful for Mart's feisty nature.

Trixie considered joining the others in the living room, but she decided against it. She would hear Brian's debate at school, since the principal had invited the whole school to attend. Right now, she wanted to get away from International Pine for a while.

She wandered up to her room and stood in front of her bookshelf. She looked over the rows of books and pulled out *Huckleberry Finn*. It was an old favorite, one she'd read over and over and had never tired of. She flopped down on the bed, opened the book, and started to read. Soon she was lost in the story. Sleepyside and International Pine were far away. What was real was the Mississippi River, the raft, and Huck and Jim.

She was laughing at Huck, dressed up in a girl's clothes complete with bonnet, when a soft knock on her door brought her back to the real world.

"Come in," she said, a little impatient at having her fun interrupted.

The door opened, and Bobby wandered into the room. For a moment, Trixie felt startled by the fact that Bobby had knocked. Ordinarily he barged in wherever he wanted to go, with a six-year-old's confidence that he'd be welcome.

"I'd like to have a talk, Trixie," he announced.

Trixie bit the inside of her cheek to stifle a smile. Now she realized why Bobby had knocked. He wanted to have a "grown-up" talk, so he was doing everything in the most grown-up way he knew how.

Trixie closed the book and laid it on the night table next to her bed. She pulled herself up into a sitting position, her back propped against the headboard of the bed, and folded her hands in her lap. "What is it you want to talk to me about, Bobby?" she asked seriously.

Bobby sat down near the foot of the bed, his feet dangling over the edge. He folded his hands in his lap in imitation of Trixie's and looked at her for a moment, his forehead creased in a frown, before he spoke.

"I wanna know about the pine company," Bobby said. "I wanna know how come everybody's talking about the pine company."

Trixie leaned her head back until it rested against the wall above the bed. She closed her eyes, trying to figure out how she could explain to Bobby something that she herself only partially understood.

"Don't go to sleep, Trixie," Bobby said shrilly. "I wanna know about the pine company."

Trixie opened her eyes and raised her head. "I'm not going to sleep, Bobby," she said. "I'm just trying to remember everything I know about the pine company so that I can tell you about it." She paused again, chewing her lower lip. Then she took a deep breath and plunged in. "The pine company is International Pine, Bobby," she began. "They make furniture."

"I know that," Bobby said. "Daddy told me that."

"Well, what else did he tell you?" Trixie asked.

"He said it's Inter—Inter— He said it's what you said. And he said they make furniture. And he said they wanna make some more furniture, so they wanna buy some land from Mr. Maypenny and Mr. Wheeler. And he said Mr. Wheeler wants to sell it to them, and Mr. Maypenny doesn't. And he said some of the people think Mr. Wheeler is right and some people think Mr. Maypenny is right. And he said everybody's getting all excited and upset about it."

Trixie nodded. "That's about it, Bobby. It sounds as if Daddy did a good job of explaining the whole thing to you. What more do you want me to tell you about 'the pine company'?"

"What I want you to tell me about the pine

company," Bobby said slowly, "what I want you to tell me is, who's right and who's wrong?"

In spite of Bobby's serious, grown-up expression, Trixie laughed out loud, scooped Bobby up in her arms, and hugged him. "If I knew the answer to that question, I could rule the world," she told him.

Bobby looked confused, and Trixie knew she'd have to try to explain things more clearly. She took a deep breath and went on. "Bobby, nobody knows who's right and who's wrong. In fact, probably nobody *is* right or wrong. They just have different opinions, because they want different things. It's—It's as if you and I went to the store and I wanted a vanilla ice-cream cone and you wanted a chocolate ice-cream cone. I wouldn't be wrong because I wanted vanilla, and you wouldn't be wrong for wanting chocolate. We'd just be different. You see?"

Bobby nodded his head. Then his forehead puckered again in a frown, and he shook his head. "When you want vanilla and I want chocolate, we can both get what we want. But if Mr. Wheeler wants to sell and Mr. Maypenny doesn't want to sell, they can't both get what they want, can they?"

Trixie shook her head. "It's as if there were only one ice-cream cone left in the whole world, and it has to be either chocolate or vanilla," she said sadly.

"Oh," Bobby said. "That's bad."

"It sure is," his sister agreed.

Bobby stood up. "Thank you for 'splaining it to me, Trixie," he said solemnly.

"You're welcome," Trixie replied. She watched Bobby walk out of her room, carefully closing the door behind him. She flopped back on the bed and closed her eyes. "Chocolate or vanilla," she said to herself. "I wonder which it's going to be."

The next morning, Trixie dawdled as she got ready for school. Although she had a constant problem with running late, she knew that this was a different feeling. The strain of riding on the bus every morning with her friends and not mentioning International Pine was getting to be too much. It was uppermost in their minds, and they all knew it, but they knew, too, that the only way to keep the peace was not to talk about it. Everyone worked hard at inventing small talk, but the lively chatter they all used to share was gone. Before, the bus ride had been too short to get everything said that they wanted to say. Now it was too long.

Trixie tried to line up some safe topics of conversation as she walked to the bus stop with her older brothers, but she found, as soon as she settled into her seat next to Honey, that it wasn't necessary.

"Guess what?" Honey asked her excitedly.

"What?" Trixie said, feeling her own excitement start to grow immediately.

Instead of answering, Honey turned to Dan. "Go ahead, Dan," she said. "It's really your news."

"Mr. Maypenny's nephew has arrived!" Trixie shouted. "Is that it?"

The other Bob-Whites all laughed. "My sibling the sleuth," Mart said, making a teasing gesture of introduction.

"I'm sorry," Trixie said. "I spoiled your news."

Dan grinned. "Well, there's more. I guess I'd better tell it right away, before you beat me to it again." Trixie blushed as Dan continued. "David Maypenny got in late last night. And Mr. Maypenny says that you're all to come over tomorrow afternoon for a cookout, so that you can meet him and he can meet you."

"Neat!" Trixie exclaimed. "Oh, Dan, I can't wait to meet him. What's he like? Does he look like Mr. Maypenny? Is he nice? Do you like him?"

"I only met him last night, and then just for a

minute, because I had homework to do. It's too soon for me to tell whether I like him or not," Dan replied. His voice was casual, but Trixie thought he looked nervous as he spoke. His gaze, which was usually direct, went from the window to his schoolbooks to a spot somewhere above Trixie's head.

Oh, dear, Trixie thought. *Dan doesn't like David Maypenny. I just know it. But I wonder why not.* She found herself looking forward to the cookout the next afternoon, when she'd have a chance to see David Maypenny and judge him for herself.

Two Visitors · 5

HURRY UP, BRIAN! Mart!" Trixie shouted up the stairs. "We'll be late for the cookout at Mr. Maypenny's!"

Brian came down the stairs, laughing. "Turnabout is fair play, they say. But I never thought the day would come when *you'd* be calling up the stairs to *me*."

"It is amazing," Mart added, following his older brother, "how her perambulation improves when a gustatory occasion, not a scholastic one, is beckoning."

"If you mean I think a cookout is more fun than school, you're right," Trixie retorted. "But it isn't the food that I'm excited about. It's meeting David Maypenny."

"We're all eager to meet him," Brian said. "And we're all ready to go. So. . . ." Bowing low, he gestured for Trixie to go out the door ahead of him.

As they walked through the kitchen, Mrs. Belden called out to them. "There's a chocolate cake there on the counter for you to take along. Mr. Maypenny is an excellent cook, I know, but I don't think he goes in much for baking. I thought a little dessert might be in order."

"Yummy-yum!" Trixie exclaimed. "Thanks, Moms! You're wonderful!"

The three Beldens went first to the Manor House to meet Honey and Jim. The two were waiting outside. Jim stood quietly with his hands in his pockets. Honey paced nervously, straining her eyes for the first sight of her friends. When she saw them, she waved excitedly.

"It looks as though your fellow sleuth is eager to check out David Maypenny, too," Brian observed.

"You guys are just as excited about meeting him as we are," Trixie said. "You're just trying your hardest not to show it, that's all."

Then, as she got closer to where Honey was waiting, Trixie burst into laughter. Her friend carried a plastic cake holder, identical to the one Mrs. Belden had sent along.

"Miss Trask was afraid that Mr. Maypenny wouldn't provide us with a dessert," Trixie guessed.

Honey started to giggle. Miss Trask had been hired by the Wheelers to be Honey's governess. As Honey had grown up and become more independent, Miss Trask had stayed on and taken over the running of the busy Wheeler household. In a way, she was like a mother to Honey and Jim, since Mrs. Wheeler often went with her husband on business trips. "Isn't it just like her to think of something like that?" Honey asked.

"For reasons I cannot explain, I am suddenly overcome with anticipation of the evening's festivities," Mart said in a dry tone. "Shall we proceed?"

Laughing, the Bob-Whites set off down the path to Mr. Maypenny's.

When they reached the tiny clearing, they saw the glow of the slow fire Mr. Maypenny used for outdoor cooking, with the big iron kettle hanging above it. Dan was tending the fire, and he waved as he saw his friends approaching.

"Where's David Maypenny?" Trixie asked.

"Inside," Dan replied.

"Will you introduce us?" Honey asked.

Dan hesitated for a moment. "Mr. Maypenny's inside. He can introduce you. David's his nephew, after all."

Trixie looked sharply at Dan. The boy lowered his head and pretended to inspect the fire. Again she was struck by the feeling that Dan did not like David Maypenny. Realizing that the others were going into the cabin, Trixie turned and followed them.

David Maypenny was sitting by himself in the tiny living room of Mr. Maypenny's cabin. When the young people entered, he jumped to his feet and held out his hand. "You must be the Bob-Whites," he said.

Jim stepped forward and shook David's hand. "And you must be David Maypenny," he said. "I'm Jim. This is my sister, Honey. And these are our friends Trixie, Mart, and Brian Belden."

"It's good to meet you," David said. "I've heard an awful lot about the Bob-Whites in the past couple of days. My uncle has told me about some of the projects you've been involved in, raising money for good causes like the school's art department."

"Mr. Maypenny was a terrific help with that project. He let us use his clearing as a rest stop for the bikeathon, and he fed all the riders, too," Honey said.

"My uncle says you also solve a lot of mysteries," David said, sitting back down.

"Did he mention that Trixie and Honey also specialize in creating mysteries where none exist?" Jim asked. "When they first saw your uncle, they decided he was poaching on my father's game preserve. Their evidence was the fact that they'd never seen him before."

"My uncle did mention that," David said. "But I think it seems quite understandable. If I saw an old gentleman in a red cap, turtleneck sweater, and knickers, I'd think he was a poacher—either that or a character left over from a Washington Irving story."

"Are you familiar with the Washington Irving stories—'Rip Van Winkle' and 'The Legend of Sleepy Hollow'?" Honey inquired, obviously impressed.

David shrugged modestly. "I know a little bit about them," he said. "I knew that my family had come from this part of the country, where those stories are set. So when we studied them in school, I paid extra-close attention."

As David spoke, Trixie eyed him closely. He certainly didn't look anything like Mr. Maypenny. Mr. Maypenny was tall and gaunt, with a ruddy, weather-beaten face and white hair. David was short and round—not overweight exactly, but kind of soft-looking. His skin looked soft, too, with almost no wrinkles, and his hair was dark. He was definitely an indoor person, Trixie felt, and he looked as though he'd never had a really good suntan in his life.

But Trixie couldn't see anything in David Maypenny's personality that would make Dan take such a quick dislike to him. David seemed open and friendly enough. His gaze was direct, not shifty. And he seemed genuinely interested in finding out more about the Bob-Whites.

"Well, I see you young folks have all met one another," Mr. Maypenny said, coming out of the kitchen. "Is everybody getting along okay?"

"Just fine, Mr. Maypenny," Brian said as the others nodded.

"Oh, Mr. Maypenny, here's a cake that Miss Trask sent over for dessert," Honey said.

"And here's the one Moms sent over for dessert," Trixie said, laughing.

Mr. Maypenny started to laugh, too. "Isn't that just like womenfolk?" he said. "Well, you tell them 'thank you' for me." He took the cake carriers from Honey and Trixie and started for the kitchen. Then he paused. "Hmm," he said. "This could be just what we need."

"What do you mean, Mr. Maypenny?" Trixie asked curiously.

Mr. Maypenny suddenly looked embarrassed. "I hate to have to tell you young folks about this, after I had to ask you to come over and help me out last week. But it seems I let the fire go out under the stew this afternoon. It was lucky Dan noticed it, or we'd really be in trouble. As it is, that stew should simmer for another hour or so. So if anybody's hungry, I thought we could have dessert first, then have the main course, and then have dessert again," Mr. Maypenny concluded, holding up one cake carrier and then the other.

"A superlative suggestion," Mart said, patting his stomach.

Mr. Maypenny looked at Mart, his eyes narrowed in a squint. "Does that mean he wants some cake or not? I can never tell what that young fella's talking about."

The others laughed as Mart blushed. "Yes, please," he said simply.

Mr. Maypenny nodded. "I'll be right back with cake and milk for everybody," he said, returning to the kitchen.

The Bob-Whites were still smiling over the exchange between Mr. Maypenny and Mart. But Trixie noticed that David Maypenny's face was wearing a worried frown. "Is anything wrong?" she asked.

David looked startled. "I'm sorry," he said.

"I—I didn't think anyone would notice. I guess I *am* a little worried."

"About what?" Brian asked.

"About my uncle," David replied. "He's older than I thought he'd be. I worry about him, living so primitively at his age."

"Mr. Maypenny can take care of himself," Jim said confidently.

"What about that fire?" David demanded. "He wouldn't have noticed it was out if Dan hadn't mentioned it. I wonder if his eyesight's failing."

"Mr. Maypenny can still bag a pheasant at forty yards," Jim said. "His eyesight's fine."

"As for his letting the fire go out," Brian said, "I'm sure that had less to do with his eyesight than with his having company for the first time in years. He was probably so concerned with talking to you that he just forgot to check it. It's perfectly understandable."

"I hope you're right, of course," David Maypenny said, still frowning. Then he grinned. "Actually, to a big-city boy like me, this type of life probably seems a lot more demanding than it really is. My uncle is probably much safer here than he would be on the streets of New York."

There was no time for further discussion, since Mr. Maypenny returned just then from the kitchen with a sliced cake, a stack of plates, and a handful of forks on a huge platter, along with a pitcher of milk and some glasses. For a time, chewing and murmurs of satisfaction replaced conversation.

When they had finished, Mr. Maypenny went outside to check on the fire. As he left, Trixie realized for the first time that Dan had never joined the group inside the cabin. She started to speak, but her glance was caught by Jim's. The red-haired boy shook his head slightly, and Trixie knew that he was signaling her not to say anything.

He's right, Trixie thought. *There's no way I can mention Dan's absence without upsetting everybody. If he's outside because he and David don't get along, then I'd be sure to embarrass David if I said anything.*

Trixie forced herself to join in the conversation. The Bob-Whites told David Maypenny about their life in Sleepyside, and David told them about what it had been like to grow up in New York.

"As I said before," David concluded, "I'm a big-city boy. I don't know a thing about small towns, and I know even less about the country." Suddenly he started to laugh. "When my uncle was building the fire for the stew this afternoon,

72

I watched him start with little twigs and put on bigger ones and then add wood, and I said—" David broke off and shook his head, looking embarrassed. "I said, 'Where's the charcoal?' I had never seen a cooking fire made of wood before. Can you believe it?"

"I can," Honey said quickly. "Why, until my parents sent me to camp for the first time, I didn't even know about *charcoal.*"

Everyone was laughing as Mr. Maypenny stuck his head in the door for a moment and called, "Soup's on! I have the bowls out here, so just come on out and help yourselves."

The Bob-Whites and David Maypenny went outside, helped themselves to hunter's stew and biscuits, and returned to the cabin. This time Dan came along and sat quietly in a corner, concentrating on his food.

They had just finished eating, and Mart was wondering whether he could possibly find room for seconds when they heard the sound of a car engine outside. They looked at one another in puzzlement. Mr. Maypenny seldom had visitors —especially not someone in a car. The Bob-Whites always walked or rode the Wheelers' horses or their own bicycles.

They listened in silence as the engine was turned off and the car door opened and slammed shut.

The sound seemed so eerie in the stillness of the September evening that Trixie jumped in spite of herself when she heard the knock on the door.

Mr. Maypenny frowned at the door for a moment as if he were trying to see through it to the person outside. Finally he got up, crossed the small room in a few steps, and opened the door.

"Mr. Maypenny?" said the voice from outside. "I'm happy to meet you. My name is John Score."

The Bob-Whites exchanged surprised looks as Mr. Maypenny said, "Well, come on in, John. We're just having ourselves a little party. Join the fun."

John Score followed Mr. Maypenny back into the room, and Trixie swiveled in her chair to get the earliest possible glimpse of the young environmentalist. She wasn't sure she liked what she saw. He was tall—so tall that the top of his head almost brushed the doorframe as he walked into the room. But he was much too thin. His patched and faded blue jeans seemed to hang from his body, and his chest looked sunken under his blue work shirt. His hair was dark blond and straight. It hung below his ears and was kept off his face by a band around his forehead. The hiking boots he wore were scuffed and mud-caked. He looked tired and underfed and dirty.

"Would you like some stew?" Mr. Maypenny asked, as if he, too, had been struck by how thin the young man was.

"Yes, thank you," Score said.

"I'll get it." It was the first time Dan had spoken since they'd begun to eat. He got up quickly and went outside, as if he were eager for an excuse to get away.

"Well, now," Mr. Maypenny said, "I guess we should introduce you around. These young folks over here are the Beldens—Trixie, Brian, and Mart."

"We live at Crabapple Farm, right near here," Trixie volunteered. "You stopped by last week and talked to our mother."

"And this is Honey Wheeler and her brother, Jim," Mr. Maypenny said.

"Wheeler?" John Score repeated, sounding startled.

"That's right," Jim said quietly. "Matthew Wheeler is our father."

Mr. Maypenny laughed at John Score's confused look. "Matt Wheeler is a mite pigheaded sometimes, but he has two fine young children. I'm proud to call them my friends."

"There seems to be something going on here that I'm not quite following," David Maypenny said, puzzled.

Mr. Maypenny turned to his nephew. "That's right. I suppose you would be getting a little lost. You remember that International Pine company I told you about—the one that wanted to buy part of my land here?" Mr. Maypenny waited until his nephew nodded. "Well, this young man belongs to a group that's trying to stop them from expanding. And more power to him, I say."

"Thank you," John Score said, as much to Mr. Maypenny as to Dan, who had just handed him a bowl of stew. "I'm glad you support what we're doing. One of the reasons I came to see you tonight is to tell you that we support you, too. We're willing to give you any sort of help you need."

"What kind of help might that be?" Mr. Maypenny asked.

John Score shrugged. "Sometimes these big companies can get pretty tough when there's a piece of land they want but can't get their hands on. If you need a lawyer, we'll help you pay for one. If you want to start looking at some ways to protect your land for future generations, we can help with that, too."

"You mean there's a way to see to it that International Pine can't get my land, even after I'm gone?" Mr. Maypenny asked.

"There might be," John Score said. "We'd

have to check into it, as I said. But under certain conditions, you can leave your land to the state with the understanding that it be kept as a game refuge or nature center or whatever. That will protect it."

"That sounds very interesting, Mr. Score," David Maypenny said. "Are you a lawyer?"

"No, I'm not. I've just picked up a little information about the law here and there," Score said.

"It seems to me that somebody once said, 'A little knowledge is a dangerous thing.' " David Maypenny's voice was mild, but John Score reacted as though he'd been slapped.

"The dangerous thing is letting our environment be destroyed by large companies," Score retorted.

David Maypenny held his hands up in front of him in a peacemaking gesture. "Don't get me wrong. I don't support International Pine. I do care about my uncle. I don't want his land taken away—by big business *or* the state."

"What have you been doing since you came to Sleepyside, Mr. Score?" tactful Honey interjected quickly.

John Score put down his bowl of stew, which Trixie noticed he'd scarcely touched, before he replied. "Mostly I've been talking to the people in the community, trying to decide if there's enough grass roots support to stop the expansion through the force of public opinion. I've also been discussing the issue with one or two members of the town council, to try to find out what our legal recourse is."

"Oh," Honey said. She looked at Trixie, wide-eyed.

"I didn't understand him, either," Trixie said helplessly.

"Let me translate," Brian said, laughing. "If he can prove that most of the people around here really don't want the factory to expand, then International Pine will probably just drop the whole idea. They need community goodwill in order to succeed.

"If the town is split, or if most of the people actually want the expansion, then they'll try to stop it through legal means, changing the laws or using laws that are already on the books to protect the environment."

"You seem to know quite a bit about the issue," John Score observed.

"I've been giving it some study," Brian said.

"He's going to be in a debate next week," Trixie added. "The whole school is invited to watch."

"If you need more information, I'd be happy to give it to you," Score said.

"I don't think you would be," Brian replied. "I'm debating in favor of the expansion."

As Score looked at Brian in surprise, David Maypenny spoke again. "Are you from Sleepyside?"

"No," Score replied. "I'm from Ohio. Why?"

"Just wondering," David said innocently. "I thought your accent sounded quite a bit different from the ones I've been hearing around here. Why would you want to come all the way from Ohio to get involved in something that really doesn't concern you?"

"Any threat to the environment concerns me," John Score said, "whether it's in Ohio or New York or—or Timbuktu."

"Don't you think the people in this area are smart enough to decide for themselves whether or not they want the factory to expand?" David's tone of voice remained casual, but now Trixie was beginning to feel uncomfortable for John Score. For some reason, David Maypenny was trying to back him into a corner.

"The people are smart enough," John Score said, his voice quiet but firm. "They're plenty smart enough to know their own minds. What they don't know is how they can fight for their rights. That's what CAUSE helps them do. We show them how to fight—legally, if possible;

outside the law, if we have to resort to that. We do anything we have to, to protect the environment—anything."

Abruptly, John Score stood up. "I shouldn't have interrupted your party, Mr. Maypenny. I'd like to talk to you again sometime. Good night."

The room seemed very quiet and very empty after John Score left. Until then, Trixie hadn't realized how strong his presence had been. She heard the car door open and slam shut and the engine start up. *I wouldn't ever want to have him mad at me*, she thought.

A Sudden Departure · 6

AFTER JOHN SCORE'S departure, the silence he had left behind lengthened. Even Honey's diplomatic attempts at getting the conversation started up again did not work. Everyone felt uncomfortable, and everyone was relieved when Jim stood up and said, "I think it's time for us to go. I have a lot of studying to do this weekend, and I'd like to get some of it done before Sunday night, for a change."

Trixie and her brothers got to their feet immediately. "That sagacious concept is one that I aspire to emulate," Mart said.

"I won't get much homework done," Trixie

added, "but I do have to get Bobby ready for bed. Thanks for the party, Mr. Maypenny."

"Thank you for coming." It was David Maypenny who replied. "I'm glad I got the chance to meet all of you. I hope to see you again real soon."

As the other Bob-Whites said their thank-you's and good-byes, Trixie caught Dan's eye. He was looking forlornly around the group, as if he did not want to be left behind when his friends went home. Thinking about the subtle way in which David Maypenny had cornered John Score, Trixie wondered if Mr. Maypenny's nephew was doing the same thing to Dan when nobody else was around.

As they walked down the path, Brian took a deep breath of the fresh September air and exhaled slowly. "It feels good to be out here," he said. "It was getting a little bit too warm for comfort in there."

"It heated up pretty fast toward the end," Jim said.

"Why did David Maypenny attack John Score that way?" Honey asked.

"I think 'attack' is a pretty strong word," Jim told her. "He was just asking some questions about John Score's presence here in Sleepyside. I think they were questions worth asking."

Brian shook his head. "I disagree. I don't want to start another heated discussion, Jim, so don't take this personally. But I think David Maypenny was way too harsh with John Score—especially considering that he himself just came to Sleepyside a couple of days ago."

"He said he was just concerned with protecting his uncle's interests," Jim reminded him.

"Then why would he start grilling Score, who claimed to be interested in helping Mr. Maypenny, too?" Brian asked.

"Maybe it was because John Score doesn't look as though he can take care of himself, let alone anybody else," Trixie said.

"That's right," Honey agreed. "He's so thin and so sort of grubby-looking. He looks as if someone had just turned him out of *his* home. I can see how David might not trust him to save Mr. Maypenny's."

The Bob-Whites had arrived at the Manor House, and they paused at the front walk. There was silence for a moment as each of them reviewed the scene between John Score and David Maypenny.

Finally Mart shrugged. "I question the efficacy of attempting to determine their motivations at present," he said.

Jim grinned and nodded. "Right. 'Time alone

will tell,' as they used to say in the melodramas. We'll see you later."

The Beldens said good-bye and turned toward Crabapple Farm. " 'Time alone will tell,' " Trixie repeated in a whisper. Then, in spite of the warmth of the September evening, she shivered.

The next day, Trixie was too caught up in the usual Sunday activity at the Belden household, including taking care of rambunctious Bobby, to give much thought to Mr. Maypenny, his nephew, or the young environmentalist.

Then, in the evening, Di Lynch called to tell Trixie that she was back from her vacation and would be at school in the morning.

"How was your vacation?" Trixie asked.

"Wonderful," Di replied. "We went all through Wisconsin and Minnesota. I'd never seen that part of the Midwest before. It's really beautiful, Trix."

"I'd love to see it," Trixie told her. The Bob-Whites had done quite a bit of traveling, going to New York City, Williamsburg, and St. Louis, as well as to a farm in Iowa, a dude ranch in Arizona, and a national forest in Idaho. They'd even visited England. But those experiences had only whetted Trixie's appetite for travel.

"Maybe we will see it sometime," Di said.

"Mr. and Mrs. Renfer, who are friends of my parents, live in Minneapolis and have a summer cottage in northern Minnesota. They love young people, and they asked me about my friends in Sleepyside. I talked and talked about the Bob-Whites, and they said they'd love to meet all of you. They said we could come to visit whenever we liked."

"Yippee!" Trixie shouted. "When do we leave?"

Di Lynch giggled at Trixie's enthusiasm. "Not for a while, I'm afraid," she said. "I just missed three weeks of school, remember? Even though I got some of the assignments before I left, I'll have a lot of catching up to do now that I'm back. I can't afford to go 'gallivanting,' as my Uncle Monty would say, for some time."

Trixie sighed. "Moms would never let me leave while school was in session, anyway. She knows I'd *never* catch up. But someday we'll see Minnesota," she concluded resolutely.

"We will, for sure," Di agreed. "But speaking of catching up, I called to find out what I've missed out on in Sleepyside, as well as to tell you about my vacation. What's been happening here? Have I missed any good mysteries?"

"Not one," Trixie assured her, "unless you want to count the mysteries of algebra, which I'm trying to solve again this year. Although

85

there is a controversy going on—the International Pine controversy, as everyone's calling it." Briefly, Trixie filled Di in on the furniture company's offer to buy the parcel of land from Mr. Maypenny and Mr. Wheeler, the resulting argument between Dan and Jim, the appearance of David Maypenny, and the confrontation between John Score and David the previous evening.

"Goodness," Di breathed when Trixie had finished. "You may not have solved any mysteries, but you haven't been lacking for excitement, either."

"I guess that's true," Trixie said, a little surprised. "It does sound like a lot, now that I tell it. But there's really nothing mysterious about any of it—except we've been wondering why Dan doesn't like David Maypenny, and why David took such a quick dislike to John Score, and whether—"

Trixie was interrupted by Di Lynch's gales of laughter. "Oh, Trixie," she gasped, "it's so good to know that nothing has changed since I've been gone. You're as mystery crazy as ever."

Trixie started to giggle, too. "I guess I am, Di," she admitted.

"Anyway," Di said, drawing the conversation to a close, "I'm glad you got me all caught up. I have to go study some more. My mother is driving me in to school early tomorrow so I can meet with a couple of my teachers. I'll see you at lunch, though. Okay?"

"Okay," Trixie agreed. "Welcome back, Di." As she hung up the phone, she thought about what Di had said. "There *has* been a lot going on," she said aloud. "I just hadn't realized it because none of it has involved solving any mysteries, except the mystery of why people act the way they do. That one I never can figure out."

The next morning, as she got ready for school, Trixie remembered what Di had said about going to visit her parents' friends in Minnesota. "That will be something interesting to talk about on the bus this morning," she said into the mirror as she combed her sandy curls.

But when the Bob-Whites were settled on the bus, it was again Dan who had news to report. "David Maypenny left last night," he said.

There was a shocked silence, followed by a barrage of questions. When had he left? Why? Had he been called back to New York?

Dan shook his head to answer the last question and held up his hand to silence the others so he could explain. "Mr. Maypenny ordered him to leave," Dan said. He plunged ahead before the second shocked silence could give way to still more questions.

"After dinner, David started telling Mr. Maypenny that he was worried about him living alone in the woods. He said he didn't think it was safe for Mr. Maypenny to be living 'such a primitive existence' at his age.

"At first, Mr. Maypenny tried to talk to him about it. He reminded his nephew that he doesn't live alone; I'm there with him. He also said that the cabin probably seems more primitive than it is because David is used to city life."

"Didn't David accept that?" Brian asked.

Dan shook his head. "He certainly didn't. He kept right on. He said that I couldn't be expected to keep living there forever, because I'd probably want to go on to school or get a 'real job' when I finished high school. He said the cabin would be considered primitive by anybody's standards."

Dan paused and took a deep breath. "Then he said that he thought Mr. Maypenny should sell the land and move to town immediately. Or, barring that, he should give David power of attorney so that if anything happened to Mr. Maypenny, David would be able to act to see that he was taken care of."

Brian whistled softly, Jim frowned, and Mart put his hands over his head as if he expected the roof of the school bus to cave in any minute.

Trixie and Honey just looked at the boys in confusion. "What's power of attorney?" Trixie asked.

"It's a legal agreement," Jim said. "If Mr. Maypenny gave David power of attorney, then David would be able to write checks for him, sign contracts, things like that. What David meant was that if Mr. Maypenny suddenly became ill or something, David, with power of attorney, would be able to get at Mr. Maypenny's money in order to make sure he was taken care of."

Now it was Trixie's turn to whistle. "I don't think Mr. Maypenny would like that idea," she said.

"He didn't," Dan said. "He said he could take care of himself without help from anybody. David still didn't give up. He tried to keep talking. Then Mr. Maypenny really blew his stack. He ordered David to get his things together and leave—immediately."

"And David left," Jim concluded.

Dan chuckled. "When Mr. Maypenny got angry, I think David finally saw that this was no feeble old man. David actually looked a little frightened. He packed up his stuff and left on the double."

The bus pulled up in front of the school just as Dan finished speaking, so there was no time for further questions as the Bob-Whites piled out and hurried to their first classes.

Throughout the morning, Trixie thought about Mr. Maypenny and how upset and disappointed he must be. He had been so excited about meeting his only nephew, and now the nephew was gone again.

At lunch, she suggested that they ride to Mr. Maypenny's that afternoon and see if there was anything they could do to cheer him up.

The boys all had chores to do, and Di had more teachers to meet with. So in the end, it was Honey and Trixie who saddled Strawberry and Susie and rode to Mr. Maypenny's.

Halfway to the cabin, Trixie spotted something lying alongside the road. Pulling Susie to a halt alongside it, she saw that it was a dead duck. "I wonder if somebody's been hunting out of season," she said, starting to dismount.

"Don't touch it, Trixie!" Honey said sharply. "It could be diseased," she added more gently.

Trixie settled back into the saddle. "You're right," she said. "I know better than to handle something like that. At least, I should know better. Brian and Jim have warned me about it enough times. Still, I hate to just leave it there."

"We can tell Mr. Maypenny about it," Honey suggested. "He can come back wearing gloves and examine it, and then bury it. That's actually his job, as Daddy's gamekeeper."

"That's a good idea," Trixie said. "Let's go."

The girls found the old man in surprisingly good spirits, although he did seem happy to see them. He offered the girls glasses of lemonade and settled down on the front porch to talk.

"I was sorry to see David go," Mr. Maypenny said. "He is my only relative, after all. I was looking forward to getting to know him better, to having him come to visit once in a while. But once he started trying to take away my independence, why, I wasn't about to put up with that!"

Trixie nodded. "I understand. I know you're disappointed that things didn't work out with David. But it isn't as if you didn't have any other family. You do—all the Wheelers and Beldens and Dan and Di."

Mr. Maypenny nodded. "That's right," he agreed. "If I were a lonely old coot, with nobody to talk to, with nobody who cared about me, I suppose I might be willing to sign my life away to my nephew just to keep him around. But since I'm not, I won't. And that's that."

Something in Mr. Maypenny's tone told the

girls that he had said as much on the subject as he wanted to.

"Oh, Mr. Maypenny," Honey said, "we found a dead duck lying on the trail on the way over here."

"You didn't touch it, did you?" Mr. Maypenny asked sharply.

Trixie felt herself blushing, remembering how close she had come to doing just that, but Honey quickly said, "No, we didn't. We just made a note to remember to tell you about it."

Mr. Maypenny stood up. "I'll get some gloves and a shovel," he said. "Then we'll go see about it. I hope we don't have any out-of-season hunters hanging around here."

Mr. Maypenny saddled Brownie, his ancient but sturdy mare, and started down the path. Brownie never went faster than a dignified walk, and Susie and Strawberry pranced impatiently behind her. Trixie and Honey spent their time controlling their horses and their desire to giggle until the little party finally arrived at the spot where the two girls had seen the duck.

"It's gone!" Trixie exclaimed, jumping down from Susie's back.

"Oh, Trixie, it is!" Honey said.

"Are you sure this is where you saw it?" Mr. Maypenny asked impatiently. "Maybe you just misplaced the spot, the way I did with that tree the other day."

Trixie shook her head. "This is the spot, Mr. Maypenny. I'm sure of it."

"I hope some animal didn't drag it off and eat it," Honey said. "It could be poisonous."

"I wouldn't worry about that," Mr. Maypenny said. "Animals are pretty smart about what's good for them and what isn't. If some animal dragged it off to eat, it probably knew what it was doing."

Trixie had been examining the ground where the duck had been. She stood up triumphantly. "The animal that dragged that duck off was wearing waffle-stomper boots," she said. "There are tracks all around here, and they disappear into the woods."

"Then it must have been one of the boys," Honey concluded, sounding relieved.

Trixie nodded. "Is Dan out patrolling today, Mr. Maypenny?" she asked.

"He's patrolling," the old man said, "but I don't think he was in this part of the preserve."

"Brian and Mart and Jim all said they had chores to do at home," Trixie mused.

Honey laughed. "Oh, Trix, I know what you're trying to do. You're going to turn this into a mystery—'The Mystery of the Missing Duck.'

There are lots of perfectly good explanations for why that duck is gone. The boys might have decided to take a break from their chores. Or they might have decided to ride through this way to get something from Mr. Lytell's store. Or Dan might have patrolled this way after all. Let's not turn it into a mystery yet.''

Once again Trixie blushed. Honey was her most loyal friend, and she was as interested in mysteries as Trixie was. If she thought Trixie was getting carried away, imagining a mystery where none existed, then it must be true. "We can ask our brothers about it tonight,'' she said. "It probably was one of them.''

"I'll check with Dan, too, when he comes in,'' Mr. Maypenny said. "If he did take the duck, I'll make sure he tells you about it on the bus tomorrow. I could even send him over tonight, if you think you'll be losing sleep over this mysterious disappearance,'' the gamekeeper added, his eyes twinkling.

Trixie laughed, realizing that the joke was on her and her love of mysteries. "I think I'll be all right, Mr. Maypenny,'' she said in mock seriousness.

"Then I'll be getting back to work,'' Mr. Maypenny said. "Thank you, girls, for coming to visit today. I do appreciate it.''

"We enjoyed it as much as you did," Honey said. "We'll see you later."

When the girls got back to the Wheeler stable, Trixie noted that Jupiter, the horse Jim usually rode, was in his stall. "Jim isn't out riding now," she told Honey.

Honey rolled her eyes. "I'll ask him about the duck when I see him, Trixie. I promise."

"And I promise to drop the subject," Trixie said. Suddenly she remembered what Di had told her about a possible vacation in the Midwest. She relayed the information to Honey, and as the girls rubbed down the horses and cleaned the tack, they talked about when and how they could manage to arrange a vacation for the Bob-Whites.

When Trixie got home, her older brothers were nowhere to be seen. Bobby, however, was very much present, and he kept her busy until dinner time.

At the table, talk turned, as it always seemed to, to the International Pine controversy. Brian had been practicing for the next day's debate, and he asked the family if they would listen to him practice later that evening.

"I'd consider it a privilege to be permitted to preview the—uh—" Mart paused, stumped for another word beginning with *p*.

"We'd love to listen to the debate," Trixie interrupted. "Have you been working on it ever since you got home from school?"

Brian nodded.

"Then you weren't in the preserve today?" she asked.

Brian shook his head. "One of the ancient Greek orators used to practice speaking by shouting over the noise of the waves at the seashore, but I hadn't thought about yelling my arguments into the trees. Is that what you're getting at?"

Trixie giggled at the mental image of Brian standing in the preserve reciting his speech. "Honey and I found a dead duck by the path when we were riding out to Mr. Maypenny's today. We went back with him to bury it, but it was gone. I was just wondering whether you or Mart had been out there."

"As I said, I was practicing in my room all afternoon," Brian said.

"The *materfamilias* inundated me with domestic endeavors," Mart added.

"Hmmm," Trixie mused.

Mart looked at his sister. "Quick," he said, abandoning his big vocabulary. "Let's clear the table and listen to Brian's debate. Fill our sibling's head with other thoughts before it fills with thoughts of mystery!"

Sighing, Trixie stood up. "All right, all right. Jim or Dan must have taken the duck. I'll give up the Mystery of the Disappearing Duck and devote myself to the Disappearing Dishes instead."

Uproar in the Auditorium · 7

AT ONE O'CLOCK the next afternoon, Trixie waited for Honey outside the school auditorium. When her friend finally appeared, Trixie waved excitedly, grabbed her arm, and tugged her toward the open door.

"Hurry up!" Trixie urged. "I want to be sure we get good seats for the debate. I hope Brian isn't as nervous about it as I am. If he is, he won't be able to say a *word!*"

"You don't seem to be speechless, exactly," Honey said, giggling, "but I know what you mean. I could no more stand up in front of the school and make a speech than I could fly."

Trixie spotted two seats on the aisle and led Honey to them. When they were settled, Trixie said, "The thing that makes this superscary is the fact that the International Pine controversy is so—well, so controversial. No matter what anybody says here today, there are going to be some people in the audience who won't like it."

Honey's hazel eyes widened. "Oh, Trix, I hadn't thought of that!" she exclaimed. "You and I know that Brian took the affirmative side of the argument just because he thought it should be given a fair hearing. The other students won't know that. He really could be getting himself in trouble! Has Brian thought of that?"

Trixie nodded. "You know Brian. He thinks of everything. Daddy asked him last night, after we'd listened to his speech, if he realized how many enemies he might have before this afternoon is over. Brian just nodded in that solemn way of his and said it was a chance he had to take."

Honey shuddered. "Couldn't he just say at the beginning of the debate that he hasn't really taken sides?" she asked.

Trixie shook her head. "I asked him about that last night, too. He says that the point of a debate is to be as convincing as possible. That means you have to sound as though you absolutely believe every word you say. He said a disclaimer—that's what he called it—would make his arguments all sound less convincing."

Before Honey could say anything more, Mr. McLane, Brian's social studies teacher, walked out onto the stage. Trixie had been too busy talking to Honey to pay any attention to the stage. Now she saw that the front curtain was down so that only the narrow front part of the stage could be used. There was a small table with two chairs on either side of the stage, and a lectern and microphone had been set up in the middle.

Mr. McLane turned on the microphone, tapped it to make sure that it was working, and then began to speak. "I'm glad to see that so many of my fellow teachers allowed their classes to attend this afternoon's debate," he said. "I think that hearing both sides of the International Pine issue will be very educational for all of us.

"There's another reason that I'm glad to see so many students here this afternoon," Mr. McLane continued, with a smile. "As you know, I am also the coach of the debate team here at Sleepyside Junior-Senior High. The debate season will be starting in a couple of weeks. I sincerely hope that many of you watching the debate today will try out for the team. I feel that the debate today will be excellent training for any kind of public speaking you might be called on to do, whether you become a teacher, lawyer, politician, or business person."

"Do you think detectives need public speaking experience, Honey?" Trixie whispered.

Honey clapped her hand over her mouth to stifle a giggle. "It certainly might be helpful for all those times when we have to talk our way out of trouble with our parents and Sergeant Molinson for getting involved in solving mysteries," she whispered back.

On stage, Mr. McLane cleared his throat. "So much for my little commercial," he said. "Before we get started, I want to tell you something about the structure of a debate, since many of you have never attended one before.

"First, the definition of terms: The issue to be debated is called the 'resolution.' In this case, it is 'Resolved: That the International Pine Company Be Allowed to Expand their Factory Operations Within the Town of Sleepyside-on-the-Hudson, New York.'

"Two students, Brian Belden and Mark Nelson, will take the affirmative side of the question. Two other students, Todd Maurer and Jim Ver-Doorn, will take the negative.

"Each side will have the chance to present its case and to present a rebuttal of the other side's case. Ordinarily, a regulation debate would take a full hour. Today, however, to give you time to get to your next classes, each speech has been cut down so that the total time will be only fifty minutes."

Mr. McLane looked off into the wings and beckoned. Brian and the other three debaters walked out, sat down at the tables, and laid out their notes and papers.

"You may begin, gentlemen," Mr. McLane said. He turned and walked off the stage.

The students, many of whom had never seen a debate, were unsure how to react. There was a smattering of applause, which did not really take hold, followed by nervous giggles.

Finally, Brian got up and walked to the microphone. "Good afternoon," he said. "My partner and I are pleased to be here today to address the resolution. The question of whether or not International Pine should be allowed to expand in Sleepyside is not an easy one. Certainly there are arguments—strong arguments—on either side. What my partner and I hope to prove, however, is that the economic advantages to the community outweigh whatever ecological loss is involved in the conversion of this small parcel of land from natural to industrial use.

"I think it's important, as we begin this debate,

to have in our minds some very important facts and figures," Brian continued. "These are statistics that represent the economic status of Sleepyside. To some of you, they are only facts and figures. To others of you, whose parents may have lost jobs recently, or who may be talking about leaving Sleepyside in order to find better jobs, they are more than facts and figures. They are a threat to your home life. They represent the possibility that you may have to leave the town where you grew up and where your friends are. They may represent a threat to your future, if your parents find that they don't have the money to help you go to college. Here are some of those statistics."

As Brian went on, listing the increased figures in unemployment and welfare, Trixie felt a rush of pride in her older brother. His low, quiet voice made him sound older than seventeen. If he felt any nervousness, it didn't show in his manner. He stood straight, his hands resting on the podium, his dark brown eyes looking directly at people in the audience.

"And that," Brian concluded, "is the story of the need for industrial development in Sleepyside. My partner will tell you how the expansion of International Pine will aid in that development. Thank you."

Brian turned, walked back to his table, and sat down. For a moment, Trixie felt upset that nobody was applauding. Then she became aware of the deep silence that had fallen over the auditorium, and she realized that that silence was a greater compliment than applause would have been. Brian had the entire audience deeply interested in this debate. Everyone was waiting to hear more.

Todd Mauer was the first speaker for the negative team in the debate. Trixie had seen him in the halls, and she had read his name in the school paper. Todd was a member of the regular debate team at Sleepyside Junior-Senior High, and he and his partner had gone all the way to the state tournament the preceding year. For a moment, she found herself rooting against him in her mind. Then she stopped herself. Brian hadn't decided to take part in this debate because he wanted to win. He just wanted both sides to have a fair say. Brian would be hoping that Todd did a good job—and so should she. She forced herself to relax and sit back in her chair.

"Thank you, Brian," Todd said. "The facts and figures you presented were very interesting. What interested me most was a phrase you used very early in your speech. You said that the economic problems in Sleepyside represented a 'threat.' Well, as far as my partner and I are concerned, it's the expansion of International Pine that represents a threat—a threat to our way of life, and a threat to life itself."

In spite of herself and her loyalty to Brian, Trixie was impressed. Brian's speech had been good, but it had all been prepared in advance. It had been exactly the same the night before, when she'd listened to him practice it, as it had been today in the auditorium. But Todd must have come up with that introduction right on the spot, after he'd heard Brian's speech.

"Those of you who grew up in Sleepyside, as I did—and as Brian Belden did, I believe—have been very lucky," Todd continued. "We have been able to fish, to hunt. We have been able to enjoy a picnic on the spur of the moment, without having to drive for miles to someplace with trees and grass. We have been able to enjoy the more relaxed pace of small-town living. Any of you who have ever visited New York, with its pollution, its high rate of violent crime, and its pressures, will appreciate the difference."

As Todd went on to talk about the beauty of the wild areas around Sleepyside, Trixie could hear a buzz start in the auditorium. Todd was winning them over to his side, she realized, but it wasn't with carefully gathered statistics and facts such as Brian had used. It was an appeal to their emotions. This wasn't the fair airing of both sides that Brian had wanted, she thought angrily. Todd only wanted to make the best showing in the debate.

She grew angrier and angrier as she listened. When Todd finished, the audience began to applaud. Trixie realized that her jaw was clenched and that she was gripping the arms of her chair. She forced herself to relax and folded her hands in her lap.

"That wasn't fair, Trixie!" Honey whispered hoarsely.

Trixie nodded her agreement, her eyes fixed on the stage where Brian's partner, Mark Nelson, was walking slowly to the lectern. Even from where she was sitting, Trixie could see that the papers in the boy's hand were shaking. She felt sorry for Mark, having to follow a speech like Todd's, but at the same time she hoped he'd do well.

"When my partner began his speech, he told you that he was going to present some facts and figures about Sleepyside. That's exactly what he did," Mark began. "The first negative speaker didn't present any facts and figures. Instead, he presented flights of fancy. He'd have us believe that the expansion of International Pine on ten acres of land would totally take away our access to nature. If you stop and think about that, even for a moment, you'll realize that it's simply not the case. It isn't all of nature. It's ten acres—ten acres out of thousands. It's ten acres that can provide two hundred jobs."

Trixie suddenly realized that she'd been holding her breath. She let it out in a long, relieved sigh. Mark was doing exactly what he should, she thought. He was getting the debate back on the track. As she listened, Mark talked about the proposed expansion. Like Brian, he had done a lot of research. He knew how many acres of land International Pine wanted. He knew how many jobs they could provide. He knew how much the company would pay to the town of Sleepyside and to the state in taxes each year.

"In conclusion," he said, "I want to remind you that these are the facts. And it is fact, not fantasy, that we must use to form an opinion on this issue."

Mark turned and walked back to his seat. Trixie began to applaud loudly, and a few other students joined in. But the loudest sound in the auditorium was that of mumbling, and there were a few boos from the back of the room.

The boos turned to cheers as Jim VerDoorn stood and walked to the lectern. The boy looked embarrassed, Trixie thought. He seemed to know that his fellow students were applauding because they expected another emotional speech like the one his partner had made. But Jim was not a debater. He was a quiet, serious student whose main interest was science, not public speaking. Trixie hoped that the audience wouldn't turn against him if he couldn't live up to Todd's speaking ability.

Jim cleared his throat nervously. "The second affirmative speaker says that my partner didn't present the facts about the International Pine issue. I agree. But that does not mean that the facts do not exist."

Jim was speaking so quietly that Trixie found herself leaning forward in order to hear what he was saying.

Jim cleared his throat again. "It is a fact," he said, "that forty-seven endangered species of plants exist in the area where International Pine proposes to build its expansion. Ten acres may not seem like much land to the affirmative speakers, but if they represent part of the last place on earth where these plants grow, then those ten acres are too much to lose.

"It is also a fact," Jim continued, "that the pollution level in Sleepyside has risen five percent since International Pine first built its factory in this area. It is true that the level is still nowhere near that of New York City. But it is higher than it once was, and it will be even higher if the expansion is completed."

As Jim VerDoorn continued, listing facts about the increase in crime in industrial areas, the possibility of water pollution, and the health problems of factory workers, Trixie found herself feeling happy and angry at the same time. She was happy because the facts Jim was listing in his quiet, unexpressive voice were the facts that Brian had hoped would come out in the debate. But she was angry because they were coming out so late.

Brian had presented the facts of the affirmative case right at the beginning. Todd and his partner had had plenty of time to tear them apart. But with the facts of the negative case coming out only now, when the debate was almost over, it would be hard for Brian to effectively rebut them.

"Those are the facts that oppose the expansion of International Pine Company," Jim said finally. "It is not a fantasy. It *is* a fantasy to think that nature and industry can exist side by side without one destroying the other." Jim gathered up his papers hastily, then turned and walked quickly back to his chair.

Once again the audience applauded, but Trixie could sense a difference in the applause. It was more respectful than the applause for Todd had been. Trixie was glad that the quiet science student had had a chance to be heard.

"He was really good," Honey said softly.

"Wasn't he?" Trixie said. Then she felt her stomach do a flip-flop. "Oh, Honey," she said, "Brian has to speak next!"

Brian had risen from his chair and was bending over the table, straightening his papers. He ran his hand through his dark hair, squared his shoulders, and walked toward the lectern.

"I want to thank the second negative speaker," he said calmly. "I am grateful, as I'm sure all of you are, that the facts of this case have finally been brought out."

For a moment, Trixie wondered if Brian would even try to counter the facts, but he continued.

"Even though I'm grateful for the facts and do not dispute them, there was one comment made by the second negative speaker that was *not* a fact. Nature and industry *can* exist side by side. With the right precautions, International Pine can complete its expansion, bringing needed jobs to Sleepyside, while doing minimal damage to the environment. Here's how that could be—"

Brian broke off suddenly, staring over the heads

of the people in the audience. In the silence, Trixie heard a commotion coming from the back of the auditorium. Following Brian's gaze, she turned in her seat and looked toward the doors on the far side of the room.

A knot of people had formed there. They seemed to be struggling with someone, and Trixie heard a voice shout, "Stop him!"

Just then, someone broke through the knot of people and ran down the aisle of the auditorium. A murmur ran through the crowd as they watched.

"Trixie!" Honey exclaimed, clutching at her friend's arm. "Isn't that John Score?"

Even at that distance, Trixie recognized the scarecrow figure dressed in ragged clothes. "You're right, Honey. That's who it is."

Score ran down the aisle as fast as he could and vaulted onto the stage. He dashed to the lectern and leaned toward the mike. "This is what International Pine calls a minimum of damage," he said, waving something aloft. "Is this what you want to happen?"

Trixie realized that what he was holding was a dead duck. As the other students in the audience realized it, too, there were gasps and stifled screams.

Mr. McLane emerged from the wings. He walked over to John Score, grabbed his arm, and

111

tried to pull him away from the microphone.

John Score held his ground. "This is what industry means," he shouted. "It means dead wildlife, increased pollution, extinction of endangered species. It must be stopped! It must be stopped *now!*"

The assistant principal ran out onto the stage and grabbed John Score's other arm. Together he and Mr. McLane wrestled the thin young man off the stage and into the wings.

The entire audience was in an uproar. The students were all on their feet; some of those toward the back were even standing on their chairs to get a better view.

Trixie and Honey, from their seats in the third row, could see everything. To Trixie, the most interesting thing in sight was John Score's waffle-stomper boots.

She turned to Honey, her blue eyes wide and her face so pale that the freckles across her nose stood out in sharp contrast. "I know where he got that duck!" she exclaimed.

Shocking News • 8

THE UPROAR in the auditorium was so great that Honey didn't even try to speak. She just widened her eyes in a look that said, as plainly as words could, "Oh, Trixie, do you really think that was the same duck we spotted in the game preserve yesterday?"

Trixie, in turn, raised her eyebrows and cocked her head to one side, inviting her friend to think of a better explanation.

Mr. McLane walked back out onto the stage, adjusting his tie and smoothing his hair. The self-confident air he usually showed when appearing before an audience was gone. He looked pale and shaken. He walked up to the microphone, cleared his throat, and said loudly, "Would you all please take your seats and be quiet!"

He had to repeat the message twice before the auditorium became quiet enough for him to continue. Even then, he had to speak over a hum of voices. "I am not going to comment on what happened here today," he said. "The young man who just disrupted our debate has been taken into police custody, and I hope that the full story will come out in a court of law. Obviously, we cannot ask our four debaters to continue under these circumstances. We ask that you remain here until the bell rings, then proceed to your next class. Thank you."

Mr. McLane turned and walked quickly off the stage, and the uproar in the auditorium began again. It seemed to Trixie that she and Honey must be the only ones in the room who were not talking about what had just happened.

Honey nudged Trixie's arm and nodded toward the stage. Following her gaze, Trixie saw that Todd, Mark, and Jim were clustered together, talking excitedly. Brian sat by himself at the table, slowly gathering up the notes and papers he had used during the debate.

Tears welled in Trixie's eyes as she realized how disappointed Brian must be. He had taken a big risk to make sure that the International Pine controversy would have an airing at Sleepyside Junior-Senior High. But after what had just happened, nobody would remember the facts and figures that he and Todd had put so much time and effort into gathering. John Score and the dead duck had wiped that out of everyone's memory.

Then Trixie's chest tightened as she realized that there was another reason for Brian's quietness. It was the Bob-Whites who had told John Score that the debate would be taking place. Trixie thought back to that night at Mr. Maypenny's. *No*, she thought, *it wasn't the Bob-Whites who told John Score about the debate. I was the one who mentioned it to him.* She let out a groan.

Honey reached over and squeezed her hand. "Brian will be all right," she said, almost shouting to be heard above the other students' talking.

Trixie looked back at her best friend, her blue eyes brimming with tears. She bit her lower lip to keep her chin from trembling. *If he is*, she thought, *it's no thanks to me.*

After school that afternoon, Brian assured his sister that he didn't think it was her fault that John Score had ruined the debate. "You just gave him a piece of information, Trixie," he said. "He was the one who decided how to use it. Blaming yourself for what he did would be like blaming a newspaper for encouraging bank robbers just because they report successful robberies."

Trixie tried to feel convinced, but she spent the evening alone in her room. She knew that the family would be talking about what had happened that afternoon, and she just didn't want to hear anything more about it.

Her sleep was troubled, filled with bad dreams about dead ducks and Mr. Maypenny being forced off his land. She awoke still feeling tired and went downstairs to breakfast slowly, without the energy she usually felt at the beginning of the day.

She found her family already gathered around the table for breakfast. Except for Bobby, who was playing with his cereal, they were all looking attentively at her father, who was reading to them from that day's edition of the Sleepyside *Sun*.

"'After Score was wrestled off the stage by two faculty members, he was taken into custody by Sleepyside police,'" her father read. "'He appeared in night court, where he was charged with disturbing the peace and fined seventy-five dollars.'"

116

Trixie took her place at the table quietly so as not to disturb her father's reading. Even though she wanted to avoid the subject of the debate, the curious part of her also wanted to know what had happened to John Score. And, as always, the curious part was winning out.

" 'The judge also warned Score to leave the Sleepyside area immediately,' " her father continued. " 'He said he was issuing the warning for the sake of the young environmentalist, who has managed to divide public opinion and create a number of enemies during his short stay in the community. The judge said he felt Score would be in danger if he stayed in the area after the incident, and he added that if Score did not leave the area, he would be taken into custody for his own protection.' " Peter Belden set the paper on the table, looked around at his family, and turned his attention back to his bacon and eggs.

"It looks as though we've seen the last of John Score," Brian observed.

"I certainly hope so," Helen Belden said. "Not that I dislike the young man personally," she added hastily. "I don't approve of his tactics, but I do think he sincerely believes in the cause he's working for."

"Then why do you hope he's left Sleepyside?" Trixie asked.

117

"I think the judge was right," Mrs. Belden replied. "John Score has made enemies since he's been in this town. There are men with families to support who have been out of work for months. International Pine is a ray of hope for them. They see Score as a threat to that hope, and I'm afraid they might resort to violence against him if he stayed in town."

Trixie shivered. She and Honey had often gotten themselves into dangerous situations accidentally while trying to solve a mystery. Still, it was hard for her to imagine somebody intentionally getting himself into situations like that, as John Score must do in nearly every community he worked in.

"Is that all the paper has to say about the debate?" Mart asked his father.

Peter Belden picked up the paper again and turned the page. "Several of the citizens of Sleepyside must have hand-delivered letters to the editor yesterday afternoon," he said. "The entire editorial page is devoted to what happened at the debate."

The Beldens continued to eat in silence while their father scanned the letters. "The opinions on what happened yesterday seem to be as evenly divided as the opinions on the expansion itself," he said finally. "One letter says that Score's act 'only proves how irrational the objections to the expansion, in general, have been.' But another says that 'Score showed in a shocking but effective way the damage we will do to our environment if we allow the plans for expansion to proceed.'"

Brian shook his head ruefully. "I really believed that a good debate would help people make up their minds on the basis of facts," he said. "I guess I should have known better. Those letters prove that nobody's interested in facts—except ones that support their own opinions. If both sides can use what John Score said yesterday to support their beliefs, then anything I'd have been able to say certainly wouldn't have made any difference."

"Don't be too hard on yourself, son," Peter Belden said. "You did an excellent job of presenting one side of the case, and from what you said last night, Jim VerDoorn did just as good a job for the other side. That *will* make a difference. Remember, the people who have their minds made up are always the loudest. But there are also a lot of people who haven't decided yet. They're the ones you and Jim were trying to reach. Don't be too sure that you didn't have some success."

Brian smiled appreciatively at his father.

"Thanks, Dad," he said. "I had lost track of the fact that a lot of people haven't made up their minds yet—even though I'm one of them. I guess the turnout at the meeting Saturday will be the best proof of whether or not our little speeches did any good."

"What meeting on Saturday?" Trixie asked.

"If you were prone to soil your delicate digits with newsprint, you would be aware of the fact that the town council will be in session this Saturday to discuss, in public and with the public, the International Pine controversy," Mart told her.

Trixie flushed, angry at Mart's superior tone and embarrassed that she hadn't read about the meeting in the newspaper. "What's the point of the meeting?" she asked meekly.

"The town council has discovered—with some help from John Score, I suspect—that the parcel of land International Pine wants isn't zoned for industrial use," her father told her. "The council has the right to rezone the land, which would keep the issue alive. They're meeting Saturday to listen to public opinion. Then they'll vote on whether or not to rezone the land."

"If the town council votes in favor of the new zoning, they're telling International Pine that the people want them to expand. Then the company will probably step up its effort to buy the parcel of land," Brian said.

"Oh," Trixie said. She felt a twinge of fear as she realized that Mr. Maypenny could be under even more pressure to sell after Saturday's meeting. She sighed. *At least it will all be settled*, she thought. *Right now, I think that's all I care about.*

By Friday, the commotion over the debate had subsided. When Trixie and her brothers got on the bus that morning, the excited din of the two previous days had returned to the usual dull roar. Even the bus driver looked less harried.

It was easy for the Beldens to spot the other Bob-Whites in the crowd. They were a small, quiet pocket in the middle of the chatter.

"Dan has something to tell all of us," Honey said as soon as the Beldens had sat down. "He wanted to wait until we were all together."

"Go ahead, Dan," Brian said quickly.

Dan took a deep breath. He was naturally shy, but Trixie could see that his reluctance to speak was caused by something more than that.

"I need some advice," Dan began softly. He paused again, then forced himself to continue. "Over the past three days, I've found five more dead ducks in the preserve."

"That's pretty unusual, isn't it?" Brian asked.

121

Dan nodded his head. "There are usually a few in the spring, when they've just finished the long flight north. This time of year, finding more than one or two a month is *very* unusual. The worst part is that I haven't even been looking for them. The five I've found were all on or near the trails. I don't know how many more there might be back in the woods."

"My advice is to tell Mr. Maypenny about it," Trixie said.

Dan grinned wryly. "I did tell him. That's the part I need advice about."

"I—I don't understand," Trixie said. "Mr. Maypenny knows more about that preserve than anyone. He should know what to do."

Dan nodded. "Exactly," he said. "But when I told him about the ducks I'd found, he acted strange. He didn't ask me for more details or anything. He just got snappish and said a few dead ducks were nothing to get excited about. Then he turned and walked away."

"Maybe he was just saying what he really felt," Brian suggested. "He's lived in those woods for a long time. He's seen an awful lot more than we have."

Dan shook his head. "I don't have any proof of what I'm about to say," he began slowly. "I—I hate to say it at all, because I wouldn't want to get Mr. Maypenny into any trouble. But it seemed to me that he wasn't a bit surprised by what I told him. That could mean, as you say, that he's not concerned. Or it could be that he wasn't surprised because he'd found some dead ducks, too. I got the feeling that he had—and that he was covering up the fact that he's actually very concerned about it."

"If Mr. Maypenny were concerned, he'd go right to Daddy and tell him about it," Honey said. "He takes his job very seriously."

"He's also serious about holding onto his land," Dan said. "With Mr. Wheeler urging him to sell part of it, the last thing Mr. Maypenny would do is let your father know about a possible epidemic."

"I see what you mean," Brian said. "If Mr. Wheeler thought the preserve wasn't a healthy place for wildlife, there would be no reason at all for him not to sell."

Dan nodded and said nothing.

There was a moment of silence before Jim spoke up. "I understand your problem, Dan. Mr. Maypenny is your boss, as well as your friend. If he tells you to ignore what's happening, you can't very well go over his head to report it to Dad. Still, it's my father's land, and he has a right to know what's going on."

Again Dan Mangan nodded, looking more miserable by the moment.

"I know we've been on different sides of this issue for a long time. Even so, I'm not interested in causing trouble for you or Mr. Maypenny. I'll tell you what I would like to do," Jim said. "I'll go for a ride in the preserve this afternoon. If *I* find a duck, I'll report it to my father. I won't tell him what you've just told us." Jim paused and looked steadily at Dan. "I'll do my best to let my father know about this without getting him excited and without making him think it should influence his decision about selling to International Pine. Will you trust me?"

Dan's black eyes looked searchingly into Jim's green ones for a moment. "I guess I'll have to," he said finally.

Trixie let out a sigh of relief. Even though Dan's problem was far from solved, what had just happened proved, at least, that the Bob-Whites had managed to keep themselves from being divided by their opinions on International Pine. Soon the city council would vote and the decision would be out of their hands. She hoped that things could then return to normal.

Trixie was setting the table for dinner that evening when Honey called.

"Jim found two more ducks, Trixie," Honey told her friend breathlessly. "He said he didn't even have to look very hard. They were just there, lying right by the path. He says there's no telling how many more there might be off in the woods."

Trixie sat down heavily in a chair by the phone. "I feel glad and sad at the same time," she said. "I'm glad that Jim found the ducks so he can report it to your father without getting Dan involved. But I wish there weren't any dead ducks in the preserve at all."

"I know what you mean," Honey said. "Jim was wonderful about arranging things so that Dan wouldn't be suspected, though. It looked like he was just going riding as usual. Then, when he found the ducks, he came home and got a shovel and a burlap bag and went back for them. Otherwise, he thought Regan or somebody might see him ride out and realize later that he knew what he was looking for."

"Jim would think of that," Trixie said proudly. She had had a special feeling for Jim ever since she and Honey had found him hiding out in his uncle's house, a lonely and frightened runaway. Jim had learned to take care of himself when he was living with his wicked stepfather, Jonesy. He hadn't forgotten how just because he'd been

125

adopted by the Wheelers and now lived in the luxurious Manor House.

"What did your father say when Jim showed him the ducks?" Trixie asked, suddenly aware that she'd forgotten about that most important part of Jim's plan.

"He hasn't showed them to him yet. Daddy's in New York City on business and won't be home until seven or eight o'clock," Honey told her.

"Oh." Trixie couldn't hide the disappointment in her voice. "Well, please be sure to keep me posted."

"I will," Honey promised.

Trixie said good-bye and hung up the phone, feeling frustrated. It was hard to believe that it had been only a couple of weeks since she and the other Bob-Whites had gone to Mr. Maypenny's and he'd told them about the offer from International Pine. Already it seemed as though the controversy had always been part of life in Sleepyside, never getting settled, always becoming more complicated. When Honey had called, Trixie had been sure that at least this latest part of the problem had been taken care of. But Mr. Wheeler wouldn't even be notified of the seeming epidemic in his preserve for another couple of hours.

Trixie was nervous and edgy for the rest of the

evening as she waited for the phone to ring. Once she even went to the phone to call Honey, but she hung up the receiver without dialing. It was important that Mr. Wheeler think Jim had found those ducks by accident. If Trixie called to ask Honey about his reaction too soon, Mr. Wheeler might suspect that the Bob-Whites had known about the dead ducks all along.

When bedtime came, Honey still hadn't called. Trixie tossed and turned for what seemed like hours before she finally dropped off to sleep.

Trixie was awakened the next morning by the ringing of the telephone. She lay still in her bed, holding her breath, waiting for someone to call to her. Instead, she heard her mother's voice continuing to talk. She rolled over with a groan, wondering what was keeping her friend from calling.

Trixie threw back the covers, crawled out of bed, and dressed hurriedly. She'd have to think of some excuse for calling Honey. She simply couldn't wait another minute to find out what had happened.

She was tying the laces of her sneakers when there was a knock at her bedroom door. "Come on in," she called.

Mart pushed the door open and stood in the doorway, leaning against the jam. "At last legerity conquers somnolence, I see," he said archly.

Trixie cocked her head and looked up at her brother, who seemed to be getting taller every day. "I *think* that means I'm awake," she said. "Well, almost. I was awake half the night wondering what happened when Jim told Mr. Wheeler about finding the ducks."

Mart nodded, suddenly serious. "There hasn't been any word this morning. Maybe they don't have anything to tell us yet. Mr. Wheeler often comes home later than he plans to."

Trixie snapped her fingers. "Of course!" she exclaimed. "I hadn't even thought about that. I wish you'd told me that before I went to bed. I would have 'conquered somnolence' a lot sooner."

Mart laughed. "Just plain asking is still the best way to get information. I can't tell what's worrying you through telepathy, I assure you."

Trixie wrinkled her nose at her sandy-haired brother. "It seems to me," she drawled, "that you should be able to read my mind, since everyone says we look enough alike to be twins."

Mart blushed. He hated being reminded of the close resemblance between himself and his sister. "Not to change the subject," he said, "but the reason I came up here was to ask if you want to go to the town council meeting with Brian and me this afternoon."

"Gleeps!" Trixie shrieked. "I'd forgotten all about the meeting. Of course I want to go! I'll have to get busy and do my chores so that Moms will let me. Oh, and Mart, that's a perfect excuse for calling Honey!" Trixie bounded to her feet and almost knocked Mart over as she ran out of her room and galloped down the stairs to the telephone.

She was just reaching for the receiver when the telephone rang, startling her. She picked it up and said, "Honey? What happened? What did your father say?"

"Oh, Trixie," Honey wailed, "I have the most awful news!"

Suddenly Trixie wished that she could hang up the phone and run away. *I've been so eager to hear the news that I didn't even worry that it might be bad*, she thought.

Aloud she said, "What is it, Honey?"

"Jim told Daddy about the ducks last night," Honey said. "Daddy called a friend of his at the state wildlife department, and the friend sent someone right over to pick up the ducks. They put them through tests at the state lab last night to try to find out what killed them."

"That doesn't sound so bad," Trixie said. "It's lucky your dad knows somebody at the wildlife department so he can get an answer back so—"

"Trixie!" Honey's usually soft voice was sharp as she interrupted. "The answer *did* come back, just a few minutes ago." Honey's voice broke and she started to cry. "Oh, Trixie, those ducks had botulism!"

An Inconclusive Vote · 9

TRIXIE STOOD motionless, the telephone still held
to her ear, staring at a picture on the wall. The
word *botulism* sounded familiar, but she didn't
really know what it meant. From the sound of
Honey's voice, she wasn't sure she wanted to
know.

"Are you still there, Trixie?" Honey asked in a
worried voice.

Trixie nodded, then realized her friend couldn't
hear a nod over the telephone. "Y-Yes," she stammered. "I just don't— What's botulism?"

"It's a disease," Honey told her. "It's caused
by bacteria—germs. The germs are an-aer-o-bic."

Honey said the word slowly, syllable by syllable. "Jim says that means they grow without air, so the swamp areas where ducks feed are perfect for them."

"What does all that *mean?*" Trixie demanded.

Honey sighed. "We don't really know yet. Investigators from the wildlife department are going to start right away to find the feeding area that has the botulism germs in it. What happens next will depend on when—or if—they find it."

"C-Can this botulism hurt people?" Trixie asked.

"*This* botulism can't," Honey replied. "There are several different kinds. The one they found in these ducks is harmless to humans. It creates an awful smell in the ducks, too, so other animals wouldn't touch the meat. But the man from the wildlife department says that where one type of botulism exists, another might, too. That's why he's going to advise everyone to stay out of the area and to avoid contact with any of the wildlife in the preserve until they've found the source and taken care of it."

"Avoid contact?" Trixie repeated. "Does that mean no hunting and no fishing?"

"Yes, it does," Honey said sadly.

"What about Mr. Maypenny?" Trixie asked. "He *lives* off the game he traps and shoots on his property."

"Daddy already talked to Mr. Maypenny about this," Honey said. "Jim went along, and he told me all about it. He said he thought Mr. Maypenny had a guilty look on his face when Daddy told him, but he said he didn't think Daddy noticed it."

"That's good news, anyway," Trixie said. "Jim must have done a good job of keeping your father from getting suspicious."

"I told you he had," Honey said. "Mr. Maypenny didn't seem to suspect that Dan had anything to do with it, either, Jim said. That didn't keep him from getting fighting mad when Daddy told him about the wildlife department's advice not to hunt or fish on the land for a while."

Trixie groaned. "I can just hear him," she said. She lowered her voice in an imitation of Mr. Maypenny's. " 'I've been hunting and fishing on this land since before you were born, Matt Wheeler!' "

In spite of herself, Honey giggled. "That's it exactly," she said. Then her voice grew serious again. "That's not all, though. He went on to say that there had never been a case of botulism in the preserve until International Pine moved in. That made Daddy mad, according to Jim. He shouted, 'Botulism is not a by-product of furniture making, you old goat.' "

133

Trixie groaned again.

"Then," Honey continued, "Mr. Maypenny began shouting about those greedy fools building their smoky factory right on the marshy area where the ducks have fed since Indian days, so the ducks have had to go to some germy swamp for food."

"Do you suppose that's really why the ducks are getting botulism all of a sudden, Honey?"

"Jim says it could be," Honey reported. "I think he's having second thoughts about whether Daddy should sell any land to International Pine."

"Oh, woe," Trixie moaned. "I thought this whole thing would be settled today after the town council meeting. Now even if they vote to change the zoning laws, Jim might persuade your dad not to sell, and the whole thing will probably start over again on another parcel of land."

"The company might decide not to build in this area at all," Honey reminded her. "That would be too bad, too—I mean, if the council decides that most of the people in Sleepyside want the factory here."

"That reminds me," Trixie said. "Mart and Brian and I are going to the meeting. Would you like to come along?"

Honey hesitated. "Daddy and Jim are going together," she said. "They offered to take me along, but— Oh, Trixie, I think I'd rather go with you. I'm afraid they're both going to lose their tempers during that meeting. Does that sound cowardly?"

Trixie pictured the big, redheaded Matt Wheeler. Then she remembered the look of cold fury in Jim's eyes the few times she'd ever seen him get really angry. "If that's cowardly," she told Honey, "then you can dress me like a chicken, because I wouldn't want to be around them, either. We'll pick you up around twelve-thirty."

"I'll be ready," Honey promised.

By the time Honey and the three Beldens arrived at town hall, the parking lot outside was filled with cars. Brian maneuvered his jalopy skillfully into a tiny parking place a block away, and the four young people ran all the way to the building and up the marble steps.

The meeting room was jammed with people, and the four Bob-Whites were forced to stand in the back of the room. Scanning the crowd, Trixie spotted two redheads in the front row. She nudged Honey and pointed. "There are Jim and your father," she said.

Honey craned her neck to see them. "They won't miss a thing from where they're sitting," she said. Then she giggled. "Nobody will miss them, either."

The five town council members were sitting at a long table facing the crowd. The chairman of the council had a gavel, which he now pounded on the table. "I'd like to call this meeting to order," he said loudly, making his voice heard above the noise of the crowd. "Before we start the discussion on the rezoning, George Gemlo, who is the head of the local office of the state wildlife department, has asked if he could make an important announcement. George?"

George Gemlo, who had been leaning against the wall at the front of the room, stepped forward. "The announcement I have to make today isn't a very pleasant one, I'm afraid. We have confirmed two cases of botulism in ducks found in the game preserve owned by Matthew Wheeler."

The reaction from the crowd was immediate. Shocked gasps and cries of "Oh, no!" rose above the rumble.

George Gemlo held his hands up to request silence. "The strain of botulism in these ducks is not—I repeat, *not*—harmful to humans. However, it is very important that we find the source of the bacteria and get rid of it. Employees of the state wildlife department are already at work on the problem. What I would like to request is that everyone try to avoid going into the wildlife areas until further notice. Your presence will only hamper our investigations. I've contacted the *Sun*, and that request, as well as more details on the cases of botulism we've found, will appear in tomorrow's paper. In the meantime, I thought giving you this information now and asking you to spread the word among your friends and neighbors would give us a head start in getting the cooperation we need. Thank you."

Gemlo returned to his place against the front wall, and the council chairman banged his gavel again to silence the noisy crowd. "All right, all right," he said. "You can talk about this all you want to when you get home. For now, we must move on to the business that brought us here today. That's the proposed rezoning.

"Now, what we're going to do is take an hour to listen to comments from you folks. If you have something to say, stand and be recognized. Then give your name and address and make your statement. The secretary will write it all down. Each person will be given just three minutes to speak so we can hear from as many of you as possible in an hour. Understood?" He scanned the crowd, waiting for questions. When there

137

were none, he banged his gavel again. "All right," he said, "let's begin."

Honey's father was the first one to his feet. The chairman nodded in his direction, and he turned and faced the crowd. "My name is Matthew Wheeler, and I own the Manor House. I also own the land—part of the land—that International Pine wants for its expansion, the land that will have to be rezoned in order for that to take place.

"I want you all to know that my decision to agree to sell this parcel of land was not reached lightly. I had several long discussions with Peter Belden, who works for the Sleepyside bank. He convinced me of the serious need for industry in this community. It was that information on which I finally based my decision.

"I also want you to know that my concern for nature and for wildlife is as strong as it has ever been. The sale of this parcel of land to International Pine is not the first step in turning my game preserve into an industrial development. It is a single step that will, I hope, improve the quality of life in this community. Thank you."

As Mr. Wheeler sat down, there was a smattering of applause—along with a few jeers—from the audience. Trixie looked at Honey out of the corner of her eye and saw that her friend's hazel eyes were brimming with tears. Knowing that

Honey felt guilty for not sitting with her father and brother to share the brunt of the crowd's reaction, Trixie reached over and squeezed her arm reassuringly. Honey turned her head and smiled a weak but grateful smile.

When Trixie turned back to the crowd, another speaker had already been recognized and had started to speak. "I've been against this expansion business since the minute I heard about it," he was saying. "I'm against it even more since I heard George Gemlo's announcement a few minutes ago. This is the first time I've ever heard of a case of botulism in these parts. I'm sure it's the result of tampering with nature. If International Pine hadn't built here in the first place, those ducks wouldn't have died. There's no telling how much worse the damage will get if we allow the expansion."

The man started to sit down, then stood up again. "I want to say one more thing. If any of you councilmen vote for the rezoning, you can bet I'll vote *against* you in the next election."

Again there was a mixture of applause and booing as the man sat down. Three people jumped to their feet, wanting to be recognized. The chairman pointed his gavel at one of them.

The speaker gave his name and address to the secretary and turned to face his fellow citizens.

"It seems to me that a person has to be a duck to get any sympathy around here," he said sarcastically. "I think it's high time somebody spoke up for us human beings. I grew up on a farm just outside of Sleepyside. My family and friends all live here. I farmed for my dad until I got married and had a family of my own. Then we discovered that one small farm didn't make enough money to support two families. For the past two years, I've been working in Tarrytown. I started out commuting. Then that got too expensive. Now I live in a rooming house there during the week and come home to my family only on weekends.

"I don't want my kids to miss the small-town life I had growing up in Sleepyside. But I don't want them to grow up without a father, either. If International Pine expands, I could get a job right here in town. I could raise my kids the way I want to." The man paused and raised his hands in a helpless gesture. "Aren't my kids and I as important as ducks?"

There was applause, but no booing, as the man sat down. Trixie could understand why even the most strongly opposed to the expansion would not want to boo him. Most of them had families, too.

The debate went on and on. Just as both sides had managed to use John Score's actions at the debate in their favor, now both sides used the discovery of botulism on the preserve. Half of the speakers said the botulism proved that the preserve wasn't safe for wildlife, so it might as well be used for industry. The other half said the poisoning of the ducks had happened because the swamp where they'd fed safely had been destroyed by the original International Pine factory. Further expansion meant risking more epidemics—epidemics that could be harmful to humans, too.

At the end of the hour, the chairman banged his gavel again and ordered the spectators to clear the room. The council needed a recess to review what the townspeople said before they voted.

Trixie, Honey, Mart, and Brian left the stuffy, crowded chamber and walked out onto the marble steps of the town hall. It was a crisp but sunny September afternoon, and the cool breeze felt wonderful against their damp foreheads.

"How do you think they'll vote?" Trixie asked her brothers.

Brian shrugged. "It's impossible to tell. The speeches in there seemed pretty evenly split, for and against."

"I'm glad I don't have to be in those councilmen's place right now," Honey said. "That man who spoke right after Daddy actually threatened them with the loss of his vote if they didn't vote against the expansion. I'm sure he's not the only one who will vote for someone else if this meeting doesn't go his way."

"Here you are," Jim said, coming up alongside them. "I looked for you in the crowd as soon as the chairman called the recess, but I couldn't see you. I thought you might have left rather than listen to all those speeches that said the same thing—or rather, the same two things."

"We were the last ones into the meeting, so we were the first ones out for the recess," Trixie said with a giggle.

"We were just trying to guess how the council is going to vote," Brian told him. "What's your opinion?"

Jim shrugged. "At this point, I don't know how they're going to vote, and I'm not even sure how I *want* them to vote. The botulism has put a new light on things, for me at least. It seems quite possible that it occurred because the ducks had to find new feeding grounds."

"What does Daddy think about it?" Honey asked.

Jim shrugged. "We haven't had much chance to talk about it. The lab analysis came in just before we had to leave for this meeting. I do know that Dad just wants what's best for the community."

"The crowd's starting to move back inside," Trixie said. "Somebody must have passed the word that the vote is about to be taken."

"Let's go," Brian said, leading the way.

Trixie started to follow, then paused. After all the talk, the decision was about to be made. She wished there were some way of knowing what it was going to be.

Even if Trixie had tried, she wouldn't have been able to guess what finally happened. When the votes were all in, it was a tie—two for, two against, and one abstention.

"Can he do that?" Trixie asked angrily when the fifth council member announced that he was abstaining.

"He can," Brian said. His jaw muscle was clenched. "Especially if he's more concerned about winning the next election than about what's best for Sleepyside."

As soon as the chairman announced that the rezoning would be brought up again at the regular meeting the following Tuesday, Brian said, "Let's go," and led the Bob-Whites back outside.

"Is this ever going to get settled?" Trixie wailed.

"It doesn't seem like it," Honey said in a mournful tone.

Trixie suddenly felt ashamed of her own impatience. Honey's situation was much worse than her own, since her father was so directly involved in the issue.

"Somebody should tell Dan and Mr. Maypenny," Trixie said. "Let's hurry home, saddle the horses, and ride to his place to tell him."

"The distaff contingent may have such liberty," Mart said. "We have chores to do."

So it was again Trixie and Honey who rode alone to Mr. Maypenny's. They took the long route through the preserve, reveling in the fresh air after the long afternoon in the steamy council room.

Each of the girls was lost in her own thoughts. They rode in silence until they had passed a shallow ravine. Then Trixie suddenly reined in her horse.

"What is it, Trixie?" Honey asked. "Is something wrong with Susie?"

Trixie shook her head as if trying to clear cobwebs. "It didn't register until we'd gone past," she said. "I saw a flash of something shiny in that little ravine back there."

"Maybe it was a crow's nest," suggested

Honey. "You know how they like to steal shiny things."

Trixie giggled, remembering plump, cheerful Mary Smith and her missing locket. When Jim had run away, Miss Trask had taken Trixie and Honey to upstate New York to look for him. There they'd met Mrs. Smith, and they had found her locket in the nest of her pet crow. When the girls had returned the locket to its grateful owner, they'd enjoyed spiced grape juice and chocolate cake in the farmhouse kitchen while Jim was picking beans for the Smiths in a field just half an acre away!

Trixie's face grew serious again. "This was something lower to the ground than a bird's nest. It must have been something pretty good-sized, too, to shine through the dense underbrush." She tugged on the reins and turned her horse. "I'm going back to see what it was."

Honey turned her horse, too, and followed her sandy-haired friend.

At the ravine, Trixie dismounted and tied Susie's reins to a bush. "You stay here," she said, patting the horse's shoulder. "I'll be right back."

Trixie and Honey both walked carefully through the underbrush toward the ravine.

"I see it now, too," Honey said. "It isn't something in a bird's nest. I'm sure of that."

Parting a final layer of brush, the girls gasped and looked at one another.

The shiny object Trixie had seen was a door handle—and the door handle was attached to John Score's battered green car!

The Car in the Woods • 10

HONEY'S HAZEL EYES were wide open in surprise. Trixie's blue ones were narrowed in a squint as she tried to figure out how—and why—the young environmentalist's car had been hidden in this out-of-the-way spot.

"Wh-What should we do, Trixie?" Honey asked.

Trixie looked at Honey solemnly. "The first thing we should do is look inside the car, to make sure John Score's body isn't in it."

Honey's face paled, and she swallowed hard. She was no longer the timid girl she had been when she'd first moved to Sleepyside. Still, she was not quite as adventuresome as her friend.

147

The idea of finding a body did not appeal to her.

Trixie, understanding Honey's fear, put a reassuring hand on her shoulder. "If you want to wait here, that's all right," she said.

Honey shook her head. "I'll come along," she said.

In spite of her show of courage, Trixie was relieved to know she wouldn't have to search the car alone.

Together the two girls climbed down the short bank. They walked up to the car and, being careful not to touch it and leave fingerprints, they peered inside.

Trixie breathed a sigh of relief that left a little circle of steam on the window. The car was empty except for a mess of candy wrappers, used tissues, and an unfolded road map.

Feeling braver, Trixie got down on her hands and knees and looked under the car. Finding nothing there either, she circled the car twice looking for clues.

"There's such a thick layer of leaves down here that ordinary footprints wouldn't show," she told Honey. "Still, I'm sure that if someone had tried to wrestle John Score out of the car, they would have dug up some leaves. So it doesn't look as though there's been a scuffle."

"What if he was—you know—beyond fighting

when they took him out of the car?" Honey asked.

Trixie's mouth fell open in surprise. "I hadn't thought of that," she admitted. "If they'd hit him over the head, tossed him in the car, and driven out here—" She broke off in mid sentence. "Honey, this is silly. We're coming up with all these fancy explanations for how 'they' got him here, and we don't even know who 'they' are—if 'they' exist at all."

Honey giggled wildly with relief. "You're right. This whole scene—the deserted car in a ravine, looking inside it for a body—had me so scared I immediately started thinking the worst. I'm getting to be just like you—seeing a mystery where none exists."

Trixie shook her head. "You can't say that there's no mystery here, Honey. John Score made himself very unpopular in Sleepyside. Then the judge ordered him out of town. Now we find his car hidden in this ravine. I'd say it's very mysterious."

Honey swallowed hard again. She'd almost managed to talk herself out of her nervousness. Now it was back again, full force. "What can we do?" she asked.

Trixie stood silent for a moment, her forehead wrinkled in thought. "I guess the best thing is to ride over to Mr. Maypenny's," she said finally.

"This ravine is on his land, and he probably rides past it every day. He might at least be able to remember the last time he saw this ravine without a car in it."

Honey nodded in agreement and led the way back up the bank of the ravine, as if she were glad for an excuse to get away from the green car.

The girls had only gone a short way down the path when they saw Mr. Maypenny, on Brownie, riding slowly toward them.

Trixie stood up in the stirrups and waved her arm over her head. She sat back down in the saddle and started to urge Susie into a trot. Then she stopped herself. Mr. Maypenny had been through so much in the past few weeks. It would be better for him if she could force herself to be calm when she told him about the green car. She glanced at Honey and saw that Honey had arranged her face in a welcoming smile. Her always diplomatic friend had obviously had the same idea.

When the two girls pulled up alongside Mr. Maypenny, it was Honey who spoke first. "We just came from the council meeting," she told the gamekeeper. "We rode out to tell you the news. It was a tie vote, so nothing has been settled yet. I'm sorry."

Mr. Maypenny stared at Honey. "Tie vote?" he asked. "What— Oh, on the rezoning, you mean. Well, they can vote all they want to. Nothing is going to make me sell out to International Pine. It's nice of you girls to tell me about it, though." He gave a little nod of his head and clucked to Brownie. "Nice seeing you girls," he said as he started off down the path again.

"Mr. Maypenny!" Trixie's voice sounded sharp. She paused and cleared her throat as the gamekeeper stopped and turned around. She hadn't meant to sound so panicky, but Mr. Maypenny's abrupt departure had startled her. He usually acted as though he had all the time in the world to talk.

Mr. Maypenny looked at Trixie expectantly as she tried to calm herself and think of a way to ask about the green car without upsetting the old man.

Once again, Honey's natural tact came to her rescue. "We had a little question to ask you before you go on with your work," she said. "We happened to see an old abandoned car in a ravine back there. We just wanted to make sure you knew it was there."

Mr. Maypenny sat stock-still in the saddle, blinking rapidly as he looked at Honey. With his gaunt features and long, beaklike nose, he looked

151

to Trixie like a startled bird. "A car, you say?" he asked, sounding confused again. "I don't know anything about a car."

"Then you haven't seen it before?" Trixie demanded eagerly.

Mr. Maypenny turned to look at her. It seemed to Trixie that his ruddy face was redder than usual. "Of course I've seen it," he said. "I patrol these woods every day. I'd see an abandoned car, wouldn't I?"

Trixie slumped in the saddle. Now it was she who was confused.

"Well, we just wanted to make sure you knew about it," Honey said soothingly. "You'll probably want to have it towed away."

"Towed? No— Why, I mean, yes, of course I will. I might not get to it for a while, though. But I will take care of it. Don't you worry." Mr. Maypenny gave another short nod of his head, kicked Brownie's fat flanks, and went off down the path at as fast a pace as the old horse would allow.

The two girls stared after him.

"What was that all about?" Trixie asked finally, speaking as much to herself as to her friend.

"I think I know," Honey said quietly. "I don't think Mr. Maypenny *had* seen that car. I think we embarrassed him, spotting something on his land that he didn't know about."

Trixie shook her head. "I'm not sure that's it," she said. "In fact, I had a feeling it was just the opposite—that he did know about the car but didn't want to admit it for some reason."

"What reason—" Honey began. Then her hand flew to her mouth. "Oh, Trixie," she breathed, "you don't think that he could be 'they', do you?"

Trixie looked quizzically at her friend, then realized what Honey was asking. "No, Honey," she said quickly. "I don't think Mr. Maypenny did away with John Score. He and John were on the same side, trying to keep International Pine from expanding. No," she repeated, "it isn't that. It's—" She stopped and shrugged. "I don't know what it is."

"Maybe Mr. Maypenny was just confused. He's had an awful lot on his mind lately," Honey said gently.

Trixie's face drained of color and she turned to look at Honey. "That's what it is, Honey. Do you know how often people have said that about Mr. Maypenny in the past few weeks? That's what he himself said when he had to ask us to find that rotted tree. That's what we said to his nephew when Mr. Maypenny let the fire go out the night of our cookout. Now you're saying it."

"What are you getting at, Trixie?" Honey asked.

Trixie exhaled slowly. "Mr. Maypenny always

has had a lot of things on his mind—hunting and fishing and trapping and gardening and making sure he has enough food put away to last him through the winter. He's always managed to keep track of all those things with no problems at all. Now, suddenly, he seems confused and forgetful all the time." Trixie paused, chewing her lower lip, fearful of finishing her thought. "I—I just wonder, Honey, if David Maypenny was right. Maybe he was able to see his uncle more clearly than we do, because we've known him for so long. Maybe Mr. Maypenny *is* getting too old to live in these woods alone."

Honey's eyes brimmed with tears of sympathy. "That can't be it, Trixie," she said softly. "It just can't be."

Trixie shook her head as if to throw the thought out of her mind. "I hope not," she said.

Strawberry shifted restlessly under Honey. "We can't just sit here all day," Honey observed. "What should we do?"

Trixie thought for a moment. "How much money do you have?" she asked, reaching into her own pocket and pulling out a crumpled dollar bill.

Honey searched all her pockets and came up with two quarters and three pennies. She held them in her open palm for Trixie to see.

"It might be enough," Trixie said. "If it isn't, maybe he'll accept charges."

"Enough for what?" Honey demanded. "Who'll accept what charges?"

"David Maypenny," Trixie answered. Seeing her friend's still confused expression, she started from the beginning. "Even if Mr. Maypenny isn't—well, failing, he *is* in trouble. If the town council finally votes not to let International Pine expand in Sleepyside, there might be some hotheads who'll think it's Mr. Maypenny's fault that they lost out on good jobs. If the council votes for the expansion, Mr. Maypenny will have another fight on his hands to keep from selling his land to them.

"David is still his only blood relative, even though they don't see eye to eye. So I think David has a right to know what's happening," Trixie concluded.

"Then the money is for a call to New York," Honey said. "Why don't we just go to my house and call? I'm sure Miss Trask would be happy to give us permission."

Trixie shook her head. "I don't think we should tell anybody we're calling."

"Why not?" Honey demanded. "If you're sure it's the right thing to do, why should we keep it a secret?"

"I don't know why, exactly," Trixie admitted. "It's partly because I don't want to have to tell anyone except David Maypenny what we suspect. I don't want to have to tell anyone about finding that car. I don't— I don't know," she concluded helplessly. "I'd just rather keep it a secret for a couple of days."

Honey stared at the ground for a moment, thinking about what Trixie had said. Usually, her sandy-haired friend's hunches were good ones. Sometimes, though, they got her into trouble. "All right," Honey agreed finally. "Let's try to call David Maypenny from the booth outside Mr. Lytell's store."

The girls urged their horses into a canter, and the restless animals took off eagerly.

At Mr. Lytell's, Trixie handed her crumpled dollar to Honey. "You go inside and get some change for the telephone," she said. "If I go, he'll ask me a lot of questions, and he'll get more information out of me than I want to give."

Honey giggled as she took the dollar. "You make it sound as if he gives you the third degree with spotlights shining in your eyes to make you talk."

Trixie, too, started to giggle. "That's how it feels sometimes. Remember when I left my diamond ring with him so he'd hold Brian's jalopy until we earned back the money he needed to pay for it? Mr. Lytell peered at me through those wire-rimmed glasses of his and asked me all kinds of questions about where I'd gotten the ring and whether my parents knew about it. I just wanted to turn and run out of the store."

"But you didn't," Honey said loyally. "You got him to take the ring, and you got him to promise not to say anything about it, even though Mr. Lytell likes to gossip more than anything. You managed to do all that because you knew how much Brian wanted that car."

"Brian deserved that car," Trixie said. "He scrimped and saved to get the money together to pay for it. Then, when the Bob-White clubhouse needed a new roof, he donated the money without a second thought. I could never be that unselfish. All I did was let Mr. Lytell keep my ring for a week. That's no big sacrifice. I never wear it, anyway."

"Well, I think it was perfectly perfect of you to do that for Brian. So—" Honey giggled again as she dismounted and handed Strawberry's reins to Trixie. "I guess the least I can do is go inside and get some change." Honey ran to the door, then checked herself and opened it slowly and with dignity.

"Honey won't have any trouble with Mr.

Lytell," Trixie said to Susie. "Mr. Lytell likes Honey because she's a young lady, not a tomboy like I am. He likes Miss Trask, too. He wouldn't do anything to Honey that would make Miss Trask mad at him."

Sure enough, Honey was already emerging from the store, holding out a handful of change for Trixie to see.

Trixie handed Strawberry's reins back to Honey and climbed down from the saddle. The girls led their horses to the phone booth, where Trixie handed her horse's reins to Honey and went inside.

First she dialed long-distance directory assistance and asked for the number of David Maypenny in New York City. She held her breath while the operator looked it up, hoping that there wasn't more than one David Maypenny. She had no idea what his address was—or his middle initial. And she didn't have enough change to waste on any calls to the wrong David Maypenny.

To Trixie's relief, the operator found only one David Maypenny, and she gave Trixie the number. Trixie repeated it loudly enough for Honey to hear, wishing she'd had her friend ask Mr. Lytell for paper and a pencil.

Trixie dialed 0, the area code, and the number. As the ringing started, a recorded voice asked her to deposit money for the first three minutes. Trixie fed most of her change into the telephone and hoped that David Maypenny would agree to reverse the charges if she couldn't get her whole message out in three minutes. Knowing herself, she reflected, three minutes would be just enough time to get him confused. Straightening out what she'd said would take a lot longer.

Ten rings later, Trixie hung up. She gathered the change as it tumbled into the coin return and went outside to where Honey was waiting.

"No answer?" Honey guessed.

Trixie shook her head. "We can try him again later." She felt suddenly tired and listless as the excitement of calling David Maypenny—of *doing* something—drained from her.

"Should we give up and go home?" Honey asked.

"I don't want to," Trixie replied. "I don't know what else to do, though." She looked at Honey helplessly. "Let's go back to the ravine," she added suddenly.

"Oh, Trixie," Honey wailed, "we already looked at the car once. What good will it do to go back again?"

"I don't know," Trixie confessed. "I just need to feel as though I'm doing *something* to help Mr. Maypenny. Maybe we'll be able to find a clue that we missed the first time. We were awfully nervous back there, after all.''

"I'm not sure I'll be any less nervous this time," Honey said. "But I know what you mean about wanting to do something. I don't feel like going home and listening to everyone talk about the town council meeting." Honey put her left foot in the stirrup and swung up onto Strawberry's back. "Let's go," she said.

Trixie settled herself in Susie's saddle and urged the horse into a trot. *That car is hidden for a reason*, she thought as she rode. *I hope we can find out what the reason is.*

The Fugitive • 11

WHAT ARE WE looking for?" Honey asked as they once again tethered their horses on the path next to the ravine.

Trixie had been asking herself the same question as they rode, and she was prepared with the answer. "First," she said, "we should look for damage to the car. If John Score had had an accident on his way out of town—even a flat tire—he might not have trusted anyone in Sleepyside to fix it. He might have decided to hide the car and come back for it later—or send someone else for it."

"Why would he hide it here?" Honey asked.

"He was in the preserve at least twice," Trixie reminded her. "He was at Mr. Maypenny's the night we were there, and he came back sometime and found the duck. He'd know how quiet and deserted this part of the preserve is. He'd know it was the best place to leave his car if he didn't want it found."

"All right," Honey said. "Damage to the car is the first thing we look for. What else?"

Trixie shifted her weight from one foot to the other impatiently. She wanted to be down in the ravine looking for clues, not up here telling Honey what to look for. She knew, however, that her friend would be less nervous if she had a definite list of things to do once they got to the car. "Second," she continued, "we see if the car is unlocked and if there's a key inside."

"I didn't even think of that when we were down there before," Honey said.

"Neither did I," Trixie admitted. "If we can get a key, we can open the trunk. We might find—" Trixie had been about to say "a body," but she stopped herself. "We might find something in there."

Honey's frightened look told Trixie her friend hadn't been fooled. "I think we should hurry up and get to the car and start looking," Honey said. "If we don't go pretty soon, I'll be so utterly terrified that I won't dare to go at all."

Trixie readily agreed, and the two girls scrambled back down the bank.

They searched the outside of the car in silence for a few moments, looking for signs of an accident. Finally Trixie stood up and arched her back to take the kinks out of it. "This old car is so beat up it's hard to tell, but I don't think there's any damage bad enough to keep John from driving it out of town."

"I didn't see anything," Honey said. "This rear tire is a little low, but it certainly isn't flat. The rear fender is dented, too, but it's already started to rust, which means the dent has been there for quite a while."

"Then it's on to step two," Trixie said, reaching for the door handle. The button on the handle pushed in and there was a click as the latch opened. "It wasn't locked," Trixie told Honey. "I feel stupid for not thinking of that before."

Trixie slid onto the front seat. Honey came around and stood by the open door, but she made no attempt to climb inside.

Trixie examined the map that was spread across the passenger's side of the front seat. "It's a map of New York State. The highway that leads to this area from the west is traced with a red marker. John Score must have followed that route when he drove here from Ohio."

"Maybe he was following it to get back to Ohio," Honey said nervously, "until somebody stopped him."

"The same road would lead both ways," Trixie said lightly. The same thought had occurred to her, but she didn't want to give Honey any more cause for worry.

"The keys aren't in the ignition," Trixie said. She lowered both of the visors above the windshield. "They aren't tucked up here, either. That's where the mechanic at the service station always leaves Daddy's keys after he fixes the car." Trixie wriggled off the seat until she was lying on her back under the dashboard. She groped around for a few moments, then shouted, "Aha!"

Trixie wriggled back onto the seat and held out a small, flat black metal box for Honey to see.

"What is it?" Honey asked.

Trixie raised her eyebrows and gave Honey a mysterious, sidelong look. "It's a magic box," she said. "Look. I wave my hand over it so, slide back the top, and—presto chango, a key!" Trixie held the key triumphantly in the air. "It's a magnetic box," she added matter-of-factly. "It's used to hide a spare key, in case the owner loses one."

"How did you know about them?" Honey asked

in a tone of complete amazement.

"Brian bought one for the jalopy right after he first got it. He was going to hide the box under the dashboard, where I just found this one. Daddy advised him against it. He said there was no point in giving car thieves a helping hand."

Trixie got out of the car and walked around to the trunk. Honey hesitated, then followed. Trixie put the key in the lock, took a deep breath, then turned the key and let the lid of the trunk rise.

Trixie let out her breath in a mixture of relief and disappointment. The trunk held a mess of papers and books—but no body.

Honey reached inside and took out one of the leaflets. "'Your Right to a Clean Environment,'" she read.

"Here's a book called 'Disease in Wildlife,'" Trixie said. "It's stamped with the name and address of CAUSE on the title page." Trixie put the book back in the trunk. "Doesn't it seem strange to you that John Score would leave all these things in the trunk? Wouldn't he need them for his work?"

"He might not have had much choice," Honey pointed out. "If he left Sleepyside by bus or on foot, he couldn't possibly have taken all the stuff in this trunk."

"That's true," Trixie said. "But why would he

165

have left by bus or on foot? We didn't see any damage to the car."

"There are lots of things that can go wrong with a car that aren't visible from the outside," Honey said. "Brian's jalopy always looks perfect from the outside, because he keeps it washed and waxed and polished. But if he weren't such a good mechanic, he wouldn't be able to get it started half the time."

"That's true," Trixie said again. She sighed. "I guess steps one and two didn't give us any new clues to work with."

"What's step three?" Honey demanded.

Trixie looked at her friend appreciatively. Honey's nervousness had almost vanished. Now her curiosity, which was almost equal to Trixie's, was taking over.

"Step three," Trixie said musingly. "I hadn't gone that far. I was sure we'd find something if we got inside the car." She looked around. "I think step three is to walk down this ravine a way and see where it leads."

"All right," Honey said eagerly.

Trixie closed the trunk, put the key back in the magnetic box, and put the box back beneath the dashboard. Then the girls set off down the ravine.

The layers of fallen leaves provided a springy

carpet under their feet, and the shaded ravine was comfortably cool. The girls felt increasingly relaxed as they walked on, their whispers giving way to normal conversation.

Suddenly Trixie stopped and grabbed Honey's arm, pointing to a small clearing at their right.

"It's a tent!" Honey exclaimed, her voice lowered again to a whisper.

Trixie put a finger over her lips, dropped to a crouch, and moved silently toward the clearing. Honey followed close behind.

Trixie was almost to the clearing when she heard a muffled scream from Honey. As she started to turn around, an arm snaked around her and a hand was clamped over her mouth.

The owner of the arm pushed her roughly from behind, propelling her the rest of the way into the clearing. A final push sent her sprawling onto the ground, and Honey tumbled down next to her.

Trixie quickly sat up and spun around. A few feet away, looking down at the two girls, hands on hips, was John Score.

"What are you two doing sneaking around here?" he asked gruffly.

Trixie stood up and began dusting herself off, buying time in which to regain her composure.

"What are you doing here?" Score asked again.

Trixie straightened and looked at him levelly, hoping her fear didn't show. "I was just about to ask you the same thing," she said.

John Score threw back his head and began to laugh. Trixie and Honey stared at him, feeling a combination of surprise and relief.

"Your question is a fair one," Score said when he'd stopped laughing. "Maybe we could exchange information. Would you like to sit down?" He gestured to a sleeping bag that was spread out in front of the tent.

Trixie and Honey sat down cross-legged on the sleeping bag. John Score sat down on the ground across from them.

"I'll answer your question first," he said. "What I'm doing here, in short, is hiding out. I have been, ever since Mr. Maypenny paid my fine and got me out of jail."

Honey gasped, and Trixie stammered, "M-Mr. Maypenny got you out of jail?"

John Score nodded. "I didn't ask him to. Dan came down to the jail a few hours after I was arrested. He said he'd gone home from school and told the old man what had happened at the debate. Mr. Maypenny said it was a 'spunky thing to do,' and he gave Dan the money to get me out and told him to bring me back here.

"I went to the cabin, just to say thanks, really.

I told Mr. Maypenny what the judge had said—
that I had to leave the area and that I'd be arrested again if I didn't.

"That upset the old man. He told me I was the
only hope he had of being able to save his land
from International Pine.

"I asked him what he wanted me to do. He
said he wanted me to stay on, to try to find some
more evidence of the damage International Pine
was doing so that he could use it to stand up to
them if the rezoning went through."

"So you've been here ever since?" Trixie asked.

"I've been on Mr. Maypenny's land ever since,"
John Score said. "I've had to move around,
though, because the people from the department
of wildlife have been sleuthing around. Mr.
Maypenny has kept an eye on the areas they've
searched. He moves me into them as they move
out."

"Have you found anything so far?" Honey asked.

John Score shook his head. "It's been rough going, what with keeping one eye open for inspectors while I use the other to search for clues. Oh,
I've found plenty of damage, from my point of
view. There's waste running into the river, and
the plants growing by the road to the factory
are turning brown from exhaust fumes. But those
things all fall within the government's allowable

169

standards," he said bitterly. "A little damage is okay with them, as long as it keeps the money rolling into the state in the form of taxes. I need to find a really glaring violation if I'm to shut the plant down or even prevent the expansion."

"We were supposed to tell you what we were doing here, after you finished telling us," Honey remembered.

"That's right; you were," John Score said.

"We were riding out to tell Mr. Maypenny about the town council vote when we spotted your car," Honey told him. "We couldn't understand why you'd left it there, with all your books and leaflets in the trunk."

"How did you know what was in the trunk?" Score asked sharply.

Trixie blushed. Searching the abandoned car had seemed natural enough at the time. Now, sitting here talking to the owner, she realized that she had been trespassing. "I found the key case under the dashboard," she told him, her eyes lowered to avoid meeting his.

Once again, John Score started to laugh. "Mr. Maypenny told me when I first started hiding out here that the inspectors would be less likely to cause trouble than you two girl detectives. At the time, I thought he was exaggerating. I see now that he was just stating the facts."

"Anyway," Honey continued quickly, "we were afraid something might have happened to you. You know—that someone who favors the expansion might have—have—"

"Done away with me?" John Score supplied. "That assumption wasn't too far out of line. I've been threatened plenty of times in the years since I started fighting to protect the environment. I've been run out of quite a few towns, and I've even been hit over the head once or twice. I've gotten to be pretty good at doing what I have to do to protect myself."

As he spoke, John Score's eyes narrowed and his thin face took on a harsh, determined look. Trixie remembered that she and Honey had intruded on his hiding place—and that no one outside this little circle knew where they were.

"What are you going to do with us?" she asked boldly before fear could take hold of her.

"What am I going to do with you?" John Score repeated, looking confused. Then, understanding the thinking behind the question, he smiled. "I'm going to let you walk back up the ravine, get on your horses, and ride home, of course. When I said I do what I have to do to protect myself, I didn't mean that I hold young women captive. I'm against violence to *any* living thing."

"Thank you," Honey breathed.

"You're welcome," John Score said wryly. "There is a favor you can do in return, if you'd like to."

"What is it?" Trixie asked.

"You can keep my whereabouts a secret," John Score replied. "Remember, I'm asking this as a favor. I'm not making a threat. You can make a beeline for the path and scream till the inspectors come, if you want to. I just wish you wouldn't."

Trixie and Honey exchanged nervous glances. Keeping quiet about an abandoned car was one thing. Not telling anyone that the owner of the car was hiding out in the woods, trying to find evidence that would stop the International Pine expansion, was another.

Trixie realized that for Honey, promising not to tell would be even harder. Her father and John Score were on opposite sides of the issue. There was no doubt in Trixie's mind about what Matt Wheeler would do if he knew John Score was hiding in the woods: He'd call the police.

Seeing the girls' reluctance, John Score added, "If you won't keep quiet for my sake, then do it for Mr. Maypenny's. I don't think he could get in any trouble with the law for harboring a fugitive, but it means a lot to him right now to know there's someone working for his side. He'd be

172

pretty upset if I had to leave town without finding evidence to stop the expansion."

"Well . . ." Trixie said slowly, looking at Honey.

"I'm putting you on the spot, I know," John Score said. "Let's put a time limit on it. I want until next Wednesday. If I haven't found any evidence by then, I'll pack up my tent and steal away, back to Ohio. Then you can tell everybody everything. But please—give me a little more time."

Still Trixie hesitated. She knew what her own answer would be, but she couldn't answer for Honey. Trixie stared at the ground, not knowing what to say.

"We'll keep quiet until Wednesday," Honey said.

Trixie looked at her friend in surprise. Honey looked back at her calmly. Her decision had been made, and she was willing to take responsibility for it, the look said.

"All right," Trixie agreed.

John Score rose and held out a hand to each of the girls, helping them to their feet. "Thank you," he said. "Now, get going, before somebody hears us talking and my time runs out before I want it to."

A Devious Plot • 12

THE NEXT MORNING, the Beldens were having a late breakfast when the telephone rang. Mrs. Belden answered it and returned to the table. "It's for you, Trixie," she said. "It's Honey."

Trixie excused herself from the table and walked slowly to the phone. She wondered if her best friend was having second thoughts about their promise not to tell anyone about John Score.

Instead, she found Honey brimming with enthusiasm. "Jim just made the most perfectly perfect suggestion," she said. "He thinks we should all meet at the boathouse this afternoon for a picnic. The weather forecaster is predicting a cold snap next week, and Jim thinks we should take advantage of the nice weather while we can."

"That does sound like a 'perfectly perfect' idea," Trixie agreed. "I'll check with Brian and Mart. Oh—and with Moms, of course. I haven't been home very much lately. I hope she doesn't tell me I have to stay here and slave away while my brothers are out having fun at the boat-house."

Honey laughed. "You make your mother sound like a slave driver, Trixie. She's not like that at all."

"I know," Trixie said guiltily. "Moms never makes me stay home when Brian and Mart get to go somewhere. I wouldn't blame her if she did, the way I'm always going off and leaving her with Bobby and all the housework."

"Your mother just wants what's best for you, Trixie. She thinks you should know how to work and how to play," Honey said reassuringly. "Anyway, we'll plan on seeing you at about three o'clock, unless I hear from you again. Miss Trask is having Celia make up a picnic supper, so you don't have to bring a thing."

"Yummy-yum!" Trixie exclaimed. "I just finished breakfast, but I'm hungry already!"

Just as Honey had predicted, Mrs. Belden readily agreed that the Bob-Whites should take advantage of the waning days of Indian summer. She also decreed, however, that Trixie should take charge of Bobby until it was time to go.

As soon as the dishes were done, Trixie took Bobby into the living room and settled down on the couch for the Sunday ritual of reading the funny papers.

But this Sunday, Bobby had found another section of the paper that interested him more than his favorite cartoon characters. "Read me this, Trixie," he demanded, holding the section up to her.

Trixie glanced at the headline. " 'Perspective: The International Pine Controversy,'" she read aloud.

"What's per— per—" Bobby stumbled over the unfamiliar word.

"Perspective," Trixie repeated slowly. "That's one of Mart's tongue twisters, Bobby. I think it means seeing the way the pieces of a thing all fit together."

"Like a puzzle?" Bobby asked.

Trixie nodded, smiling wryly. "International Pine is a lot like a puzzle, Bobby."

"You said it was like an ice-cream cone," Bobby said accusingly. "You said International Pine only had one ice-cream cone, and it was chocolate or vanilla but not both."

176

Trixie groaned, remembering that earlier conversation. She'd been so proud of herself for putting the controversy into terms Bobby could understand. Now she realized that he'd taken every word she had said at face value. Impulsively, she reached over and gave her younger brother a hug.

Bobby quickly wriggled out of her arms. "Read to me," he said insistently, pointing at the article.

"This part isn't funny, like the cartoons, Bobby," Trixie said. "Wouldn't you rather hear the cartoons?"

Bobby stuck his lower lip out stubbornly. "This part first, *then* the cartoons," he said.

Trixie sighed. The last thing she wanted to do was to read another rehash of the International Pine issue. On the other hand, reading was one of the least taxing things to do with Bobby. At least he couldn't skin his knees or get his clothes dirty while being read to.

" 'Perspective: The International Pine Controversy,' " Trixie began again.

The section consisted mostly of pictures with short captions. There was a picture of the original International Pine factory and an aerial photograph of the land where they wanted to build the expansion. There were pictures of John

Score being led off to jail, of Matt Wheeler speaking at the town council meeting, and of the council chairman announcing the tie vote.

Trixie found her own interest mounting as Bobby's attention started to wander. *Mart is right*, she thought. *I should pay more attention to the newspaper.*

Just then Bobby asked, "Where's the ice-cream cones? How come there's no pictures of ice-cream cones?"

Trixie, laughing, put away the news section and read Bobby the comics.

When the Bob-Whites were all assembled at the boathouse that afternoon, Trixie told them about Bobby's misunderstanding.

Her friends laughed until the tears rolled down their faces. "Poor Trixie!" Di Lynch gasped. "I can just imagine you thinking you'd cleared the whole thing up for Bobby, only to find out that you'd actually steered him clear away from the whole issue. That happens to me with the twins all the time." Di had a set of twin brothers who were just Bobby's age, as well as a younger set of twin sisters.

"Nonetheless," Mart said, "it was an excellent analogy. I am amazed by your perspicuity, my dear Beatrix."

Trixie blushed. She knew that Mart's compliment must be genuine, because he'd balanced it by using her hated real name. "You think I'm clever because I used food for the comparison—and *that's* always your favorite issue," she retorted.

After the laughter over Trixie's remark had subsided, Honey suggested that the Bob-Whites organize a game of volleyball. "If you could see how much food Celia packed in that picnic basket," Honey said, "you'd know how important it is that we work up huge appetites."

"My current gustatory desires would no doubt suffice," Mart said. "But since physical exertion will not diminish them, I would be delighted to take part."

Jim quickly got up and busied himself with putting up the net between two trees. Trixie watched him curiously. Because of their special friendship, she and Jim were sensitive to one another's moods. She couldn't read his thoughts as she could Honey's, but she knew when something was bothering him. Something was obviously bothering him this afternoon. He'd hardly spoken since the Beldens had arrived at the boathouse, and even his laughter had seemed preoccupied. Trixie hoped that Jim would tell them what was on his mind, but she knew that no amount of urging would get him to do so until he was ready.

Trixie stood up, brushed herself off, and walked to the net. "Girls against boys?" she asked, picking up the ball and twirling it challengingly.

"Why, Trixie, you surprise me," Brian said mockingly. "I always thought you liked to *win*. Now here you are, practically requesting a chance to lose."

Trixie pretended to throw the ball at Brian's head, and he ducked, grinning.

"Brian's right," Jim said. "He and Mart and Dan and I have a height advantage, and we outnumber you."

Trixie looked questioningly at Jim. It definitely wasn't like him not to go along with a joke.

Under Trixie's probing gaze, Jim seemed suddenly to realize that her challenge *had* been a joke. Flustered, he tried to recover. "I'll tell you what," he said. "We will graciously consent to *lend* you one of our esteemed selves for the duration of the game. How about it, guys? Who wants to be an honorary girl?"

Mart groaned and turned his back to avoid being picked. Dan grinned shyly. Brian shrugged and walked to the other side of the net. "I've always wanted to see how the other half lives," he said.

"All set?" Trixie asked, looking around at her teammates. "Volley for serve," she said, tossing the ball into the air.

A half hour later, the seven red-faced, exhausted Bob-Whites collapsed on the ground around the picnic basket.

"I don't think I like being a girl," Brian panted. "It's too tiring."

"Being a boy isn't exactly relaxing when it means playing against female demons like you," Dan replied.

"At least we won," Jim said.

"Only by two points," Honey retorted. "If I were two inches taller, you wouldn't have won at all."

"Cease and desist!" Mart ordered. "We do not need post-competition commentary. We need sustenance!"

Trixie rose to her knees and crawled to the picnic basket. "If you want to eat, you'd better help us unpack the lunch," she threatened, handing Mart a bundle of plastic knives, forks, and spoons.

It took only a few minutes to have Celia's well-packed lunch spread out on the blanket. She had included roast beef and chicken sandwiches, vegetables and dip, potato salad, and a luscious angel food cake for dessert.

Mart grabbed a sandwich with each hand as soon as Di had removed the foil covering from the plate. He looked from one to the other as if he couldn't figure out where to start. Finally, he took a huge bite out of the chicken sandwich, chewed and swallowed, then rolled his eyes to express his happiness before taking a bite of roast beef.

"Celia's picnic lunches are super scrumptious, aren't they?" Honey asked, helping herself to potato salad and a single sandwich.

Trixie nodded, her mouth too full to speak. She was watching Jim, who had waited until the others started eating before helping himself to the food. Now he was staring at his full plate, poking holes in his potato salad with his fork.

Trixie swallowed and started to take another bite. Instead, she put her fork back on her plate and blurted impulsively, "Jim, what's been bothering you all day?"

Jim looked up, startled. An angry look crossed his face, as if he felt his privacy had been invaded. Then he smiled. "I can't fool you, can I, Trixie? Something *has* been bothering me, but I'm not sure I should tell you about it."

"Why not?" Trixie demanded.

"Oh, Jim, you can tell us," Honey urged. "We have to trust one another, or there's no point in even having a club like the Bob-Whites."

Jim hesitated. "I suppose you're right. I've been holding back partly because I didn't want to worry you. Now that you *know* I'm holding back, you'll probably worry even more if I don't tell. You have to promise to keep this a secret, though."

"We promise," Trixie said quickly. "What is it?"

Jim set down his plate and folded his hands. "Just after Honey called you about the cookout, I got a call from the head of the state wildlife department. He asked if he could come out to the house and talk to me. When he got there, he had a map with him. The map shows the locations of all the ducks that have been found by the inspectors. He asked me to show him where I'd found those first two ducks we sent to the lab.

"He marked those two places on the map, then he held the map up and told me to take a look at it. He asked me if there was anything that struck me right away."

"Was there?" Trixie asked as Jim paused for a moment.

Jim nodded. "It didn't take an expert to spot it. I found two ducks Friday night. The inspectors found three on Saturday morning and three more this morning. The two I found were a hundred

183

feet apart. That's just about how much distance separated the three the inspectors found yesterday and today. On the map, it looks like three sets of ducks—all close together and all near a path."

"Do you mean the inspector thinks his crew isn't doing a very good job of finding the ducks?" Di Lynch asked.

Jim shook his head. "His people are experts. If that's all they found, it means that's all there were."

"That sounds like good news to me," Dan said. "The ducks I found were close to the path, too. I figured that meant there were a lot down in the woods. If there aren't, it means the epidemic is smaller than we thought."

"It means there isn't an epidemic at all!" Jim almost shouted, his patience exhausted by his friends' interruptions. "The department head is almost sure those ducks are being planted!"

There was a moment of silence before Di Lynch said, "Oh, Jim, I'm sorry, but I still don't understand."

Jim smiled at her gently. "I'm the one who should be sorry—for shouting like that. I guess the news was upsetting me more than I'd realized. It's probably good that I got it out. Maybe now I can explain calmly."

Jim took a deep breath before he continued. "The ducks are being planted. Somebody, somehow, has got hold of a small quantity of botulism toxin. They're inoculating the ducks with it and putting them in the woods after they're dead—putting them close to the paths so they'll be found."

"That toxin can't be easy to get," Brian observed.

"It isn't," Jim said. "That, in a way, is the best break in the case so far. Only a few labs across the country keep a supply. If a check shows that any of it has been stolen recently, it will put us that much closer to finding out who the culprit is."

"I still don't understand," Di Lynch said, tossing her long black hair. "Why would somebody plant the ducks?"

"There are two possibilities," Jim said, "as there are in everything having to do with the International Pine expansion.

"One possibility is that somebody who favors the expansion wants to destroy the preserve's value as a game refuge. The other possibility is that someone who opposes the expansion wants to make International Pine look bad, by making it look as though it's their factory that's causing the 'epidemic.' "

Trixie suddenly felt as though she'd been kicked in the stomach. She knew someone who wanted to make International Pine look bad. That someone had a book on wildlife diseases that would probably tell all about botulism. That someone was hiding out in the preserve—and she and Honey had promised not to tell anyone that he was there! Trixie sneaked a look at Honey and saw that her friend was thinking the same thing.

"What are you thinking, Trixie?" Jim asked sharply.

Trixie looked up and saw Jim's green eyes looking back at her suspiciously. She blushed and tried frantically to think of something to say.

"Trixie is just shocked to think that someone would murder those poor ducks in order to prove their own point of view. Isn't that right, Trixie?" Honey prompted.

Trixie gulped and nodded silently.

"It's bad news, all right," Brian said. "I just hope they catch whoever it is—and soon."

Suddenly Trixie stood up. "I—I don't feel much like eating cake right now," she said truthfully. "I think I'll go home. Honey, would you walk with me?"

"Of course," Honey said, scrambling to her feet. "Di, would you mind very much staying here and helping the boys pack the picnic basket?

They'll never manage to do it without spilling or breaking something."

Di nodded, but her violet eyes reflected her hurt at being left out.

Trixie walked away as slowly as her impatience would allow. As soon as they were out of sight—and hearing—of the others, she stopped and turned to Honey, grabbing both of her arms. "John Score is poisoning those ducks," she said in a rasping whisper.

Honey's hazel eyes brimmed with tears. "Oh, Trix, I know! I knew it as soon as Jim said it could be somebody who opposes the expansion. What are we going to do?"

"We have to catch him in the act. Don't you see, Honey? We promised not to tell anybody we saw John Score in the woods. We didn't promise not to tell anyone we saw him planting dead ducks. If we catch him red-handed, we can tell the wildlife department inspectors about it without breaking our promise."

Honey nodded. "I can understand that," she said. "But I don't understand how we can catch him."

Trixie thought for a moment. "We'll sneak out late tonight and go to his camp. Then we'll just wait. He must plant those ducks at night; that's the only time those woods aren't swarming with

187

inspectors. If we wait long enough, we'll see something that will prove he's guilty. I just know it."

A few moments later the girls parted, having made plans to meet on the path after dark.

Terror! • 13

THAT NIGHT, Trixie waited at the meeting place for several minutes before Honey appeared. She was beginning to wonder if her friend had been unable to leave the house when she heard the Bob-White whistle—*bob, bob-white*—that Jim had taught them.

Trixie whistled back, and soon Honey was at her side. "I'd almost given up," whispered Trixie.

"Mother and Daddy were talking in the library. I was afraid I wouldn't be able to get past them, so I waited," Honey told her.

"Did they hear you leave?" Trixie asked.

Honey shook her head. "I finally went downstairs, thinking I could just say I was getting a glass of milk, and I saw that the library doors were closed. No sound can get through them."

Trixie nodded, remembering the heavy wooden doors to the library at the Manor House.

"What do we do now?" Honey asked.

"We'll just walk down the path until we come to the ravine where John Score's car is hidden," Trixie said. "Go slowly and keep your eyes open. We don't want to run into him accidentally, as we did the other day."

The girls walked on without speaking, trying not to make any noise. Once or twice they tripped over tree roots growing in the path, and Trixie wished silently that she'd remembered to bring a flashlight.

The girls were almost to the ravine when they heard the sound of a car coming toward them. They looked at each other in surprise—the woods were usually deserted at this time of night.

"I bet it's him," Trixie whispered. "He may already have planted the ducks and be coming back. Hide!"

The girls darted off the path and hid themselves behind some bushes. They strained their eyes in the darkness, expecting to see John Score's battered green car.

What they saw instead was a shiny new car with New York State license plates. As the car passed them, Trixie recognized the driver. "It's David Maypenny!" she exclaimed. She ran out into the road and waved her arms.

The car slowed, then stopped. Trixie ran up alongside it, with Honey following close behind her. Trixie stuck her head through the open window on the passenger's side of the car. "Hello!" she said, then drew her head back involuntarily as a strange smell struck her. "Whew!" she said. "What's that?"

"Nothing," David Maypenny snapped. "I mean, there's nothing in here now. I—I forgot a sandwich on the backseat for a couple of days."

"Oh," Trixie said.

"We're really glad to see you," Honey told David. "We tried to call you the other day, but there was no answer."

"You called me? Where?" David Maypenny had turned snappish again.

"In New York City," Honey told him. "We got your number from directory assistance."

"Of course," David said, trying to sound jovial but not quite succeeding.

I wonder what he's so nervous about, Trixie thought. Aloud she said, "Mr. Maypenny is in a lot of trouble because of this International Pine

191

issue. We thought you should be here with him. That's why we're glad to see you—because you obviously had the same idea."

"That's it, of course," David said. "I thought I should come and have another try at making peace with my uncle. There's no point in letting one little disagreement come between us, now, is there?"

As David spoke, Trixie found herself wondering again about the strange smell in his car. The smell of a spoiled sandwich wouldn't linger so strongly after it had been thrown out. She peered through the darkness into the backseat. There was a burlap bag tied with rope and filled with something lumpy.

"What are you looking at?" David Maypenny barked.

Trixie looked up so fast that she bumped her head on the top of the window. Suddenly she realized what was happening, as if the jolt had caused all the pieces to fall into place: the funny smell, the burlap bag, David Maypenny's appearance in the woods late at night. . . .

"Ducks!" she said. "You have ducks in that bag. You killed them with botulism, and now you're here to plant them!"

David Maypenny's eyes filled with rage, and Trixie knew for certain that she was right. She

192

saw him reach for the door handle.

"Run, Honey!" Trixie shouted, giving her friend a shove as David Maypenny got out of the car. Trixie started down the path full speed. Then she heard a crashing noise and realized that Honey hadn't followed her. She'd taken off through the woods instead. Trixie stopped and looked over her shoulder. David Maypenny was standing beside his car. He looked at Trixie, who was already several yards down the path, and then he looked in the direction Honey had taken. Finally, he charged into the woods.

Trixie froze for a moment, wondering what to do. She didn't want to leave Honey alone, with David Maypenny chasing her, but she knew that the two of them against a grown man would not be an even contest, either.

Then another thought struck her, and she took off full speed down the path, running toward the ravine.

When she reached it, she scrambled down the bank. "Please be there," she breathed, running toward John Score's tent.

John Score was sound asleep in his sleeping bag outside the tent. Trixie knelt beside him and shook him. "Wake up, please!" she shouted. "Help!"

John Score sat bolt upright and blinked at

Trixie. "What is it?" he asked. "What's wrong?"

Out of breath from running, Trixie could only gasp, "The ducks— The man— He has Honey!"

John Score seemed to understand immediately. "Where?" he asked.

Trixie pointed down the path.

He threw back the sleeping bag and stood up, revealing the same ragged jeans he had been wearing the first time Trixie saw him.

He ran to the car, with Trixie following behind him. He got in behind the wheel and Trixie collapsed on the passenger's side.

John Score turned the ignition key, put the car in reverse, and floored the accelerator. With a roar, the car lurched up the bank to the path, scattering camouflage branches in its wake.

Throwing the car into forward gear, Score took off down the path. In seconds, they reached David Maypenny's car. Trixie, still gasping for breath, was stunned. It had seemed to her that she'd run miles to get to the ravine. Actually it had been only a few hundred yards.

John Score stepped on the brakes, and the car skidded to a halt. He slammed the car into park. "Which way?" he demanded.

Trixie pointed to the side of the road where Honey and David Maypenny had disappeared. John Score, followed closely by Trixie, got out of the car and started toward the spot. Then he stopped, hearing noises coming toward them from the woods.

Trixie watched in horror as David Maypenny reappeared. He was holding a kicking and struggling Honey tightly by one of her slender arms.

David Maypenny glanced up from the struggle and saw John Score watching him. For a moment, he too stood motionless.

For a few seconds that seemed like hours, everything was still. John Score and David Maypenny stared at each other. Trixie watched breathlessly. Even Honey stopped struggling and waited for something to happen.

Finally, John Score took a step forward. David Maypenny looked from him to Honey, then shoved the girl away from him and disappeared back into the woods. John Score ran after him.

Trixie hurried to Honey's side. "Are you all right?" she asked.

Honey nodded silently, her breath coming in tortured gasps.

Without thinking, Trixie turned and started to run. She ran back down the path toward home. Her frenzied mind couldn't form a plan. She only knew that she had to find help somewhere, somehow.

Again it seemed as though she had run for

195

miles, and she wondered how long she could keep going. Then she saw the headlights of a car. She stopped in the middle of the road and waved her arms over her head to stop it. She felt a twinge of fear, wondering if the car were being driven by an accomplice of David Maypenny's, but she was too tired to care. She only knew she couldn't run any farther.

As the car stopped, Trixie was dimly aware that it was black and white. *Police!* she thought happily. The door on the passenger's side opened and strong arms pulled her inside. The car started up again immediately, speeding down the path to the place where Honey was waiting.

Trixie looked up at the person sitting next to her. "Jim!" she exclaimed. "How did you—"

"I'll explain that later," Jim said. "Is Honey all right?"

Trixie nodded, then gulped. Honey was all right, but it was no thanks to Trixie. Now that the danger was almost past, Trixie realized, as she always did, what a close escape she'd had.

The police car, with Sergeant Molinson at the wheel, pulled up behind David Maypenny's car just as John Score was hauling the culprit out of the woods.

"Let go of that man!" Sergeant Molinson ordered.

Trixie ran to the policeman. "No, no!" she shouted. "You don't understand! It's the other one! Arrest *him!*"

Sergeant Molinson stared at Trixie in amazement. Then he looked back at John Score and David Maypenny. "I don't know what's going on here," he said, "but we're going to find out back at the station. You're *both* under arrest." Another squad car had pulled up behind Molinson's, and as the two policemen got out, the sergeant motioned them toward Score and Maypenny.

"No—" Trixie protested.

Sergeant Molinson turned on her. "You be at the station at eight o'clock tomorrow morning. I'll listen to your story then. From past experience, I'd say it will be a very entertaining one. But if you say one more word tonight, I'll arrest you, too!"

Trixie could tell Sergeant Molinson was angry enough to carry out his threat. She looked helplessly at John Score. To her surprise, he was grinning broadly. He could take care of himself, she realized. At least he wouldn't be in real trouble once the whole story came out.

Then she looked at David Maypenny. He *was* in real trouble, and he looked as if he knew it. Sergeant Molinson's men were putting handcuffs on him, and he put up no resistance. *He looks almost as if he's going to cry*, Trixie thought.

Honey had run over to the police car, where she was hugged by Jim—and, Trixie saw with surprise, by Mart and Brian. *They must have been in the backseat all along*, Trixie thought. In the excitement, she hadn't even noticed.

"You have some explaining to do, as usual," Brian told her sternly.

Trixie looked at the ground. "I know," she said. "Daddy will be furious. So will Moms. I don't think Sergeant Molinson is very happy with me, either."

"Oh, Trixie, that isn't the worst part," Honey wailed.

Trixie looked up. Honey's blond hair was a tangled mess, with twigs and leaves still stuck in it from her race through the woods. Her face was dirtier than Trixie had ever seen it, and tears were coursing down through the dirt, leaving streaks.

"What is it, Honey?" Trixie asked.

"S-Somebody has to tell Mr. Maypenny that his nephew is a criminal!" Honey sobbed.

At the Police Station • 14

TRIXIE TURNED PALE. "Oh, woe," she moaned. "I thought everything was taken care of, just because we found out who's been poisoning the ducks. I didn't think about Mr. Maypenny. How can we break the news to him?"

"There's only one piece of news you'll be breaking yet tonight," Sergeant Molinson said. "That's the news that you're safe and sound, which your parents are waiting to hear. There's time enough to deal with the rest of it in the morning."

The sergeant herded the Bob-Whites into his car while his men took John Score and David

Maypenny off to the police station.

"How did you find us?" Trixie asked as they started off on the path toward home.

"You found us, remember?" Jim teased.

"Oh, Jim, you know what she means," Honey said, too exhausted to be tactful. "Why were you boys riding down this path with Sergeant Molinson in the first place?"

"I was in my room studying, and I started thinking about the way you girls had acted at the boathouse when I told you those ducks had been planted," Jim explained. "I had a feeling you knew more than you were telling. I went to your room, Honey, to ask you about it, and you weren't there. I looked all over the house, then I called the Beldens—"

"That's when we discovered that Trixie was missing, as well," Brian supplied.

"Based on your previously exhibited penchant for misadventure, we surmised it was time to phone the constabulary," Mart added.

"Since it was your reaction to the news about the ducks that had made me suspicious in the first place, the preserve seemed like the logical place to start looking," Jim said.

"I doubt that we'd have got to you in time if you hadn't come running down the path," Brian said soberly.

"What do you suppose—" Trixie stopped short. She wanted to ask what David Maypenny would have done to them if Sergeant Molinson—and John Score—hadn't been around, but she decided it would be better if Honey didn't know.

"What were you going to say, Trix?" Jim asked.

Trixie yawned broadly. "Never mind," she replied sleepily.

Back home, Trixie let Brian and Mart give their parents the story of the night's happenings. When they were finished, her father turned to her, a stern expression on his face. Trixie was too tired to dread the coming lecture, however. Seeing her drooping eyelids, Peter Belden sighed. "You'd better get some sleep," he said. "We'll discuss this further tomorrow morning."

Trixie nodded silently and half-stumbled up the stairs to her room. Moments later, as she was drifting off to sleep, she felt a twinge of sadness as she remembered that though her ordeal was over, Mr. Maypenny's worst moment was yet to come.

The next morning, Brian, Mart, and Trixie drove to the Manor House in Brian's jalopy to pick up Honey and Jim. Honey came out of the house alone.

"Jim isn't coming with us," Honey said with a

201

frown as she settled into the backseat next to Trixie. "He was very mysterious about where he *was* going. All he would say was that he had more important things to do than listen to us being scolded by Sergeant Molinson for the umpteenth time."

"I don't think that's very mysterious," Trixie said ruefully. "I'd miss the scolding, too, if I could."

When the four Bob-Whites entered Sergeant Molinson's office, they found it already crowded with people. Looking around, Trixie saw the sergeant, John Score, Mr. Maypenny, Dan Mangan, and a man she didn't know.

Mr. Maypenny smiled at Honey and Trixie. *Oh, woe,* Trixie thought. *He still doesn't know about his nephew. I wish I didn't have to be around when he finds out.*

"Good morning," Sergeant Molinson said cheerfully. "I hope you had a good night's rest. Now, if you'll be seated, I will fill you in on the story behind what happened last night."

Trixie looked at the policeman suspiciously, wondering why he seemed so glad to see them— and why he was offering information instead of his usual warning not to get involved in police business.

"First of all," the sergeant said, gesturing toward

the stranger in the room, "I'd like you to meet David Maypenny."

"Wh-What?" Trixie stammered, looking from the sergeant to the stranger to Mr. Maypenny, who was still smiling happily.

"That's right," Molinson said. "This is Mr. Maypenny's real nephew."

"Then who is—" Trixie gestured vaguely, not knowing what to call this man she had thought of as "David Maypenny."

"He's an imposter," Sergeant Molinson said. "His real name is Lawrence Howard, and he's wanted for fraud in five states."

"Ahhh," Trixie breathed. Suddenly she realized why Sergeant Molinson was so cheerful this morning. Capturing a man who was wanted in five states would make any policeman happy.

"Wh-What did he do in all those states?" Honey asked fearfully.

"He's never been charged with a violent crime," the sergeant told her reassuringly. "But the crimes he's committed are about as low as they can get. It's the same scheme he tried to pull here in Sleepyside.

"He preyed on lonely old people with no families. He'd get some information about them, then pose as a long-lost relative. He'd convince them that they should turn over their property and money to him, so that he could take care of them in case of an emergency. Then he'd vanish, leaving them broke."

"That's horrible!" Honey breathed.

Sergeant Molinson nodded. "It is that," he said. "Fortunately, he stashed most of his money away—maybe he wanted security for his own old age—so we'll be able to return some of it to his victims."

"None of what you've said explains why Howard planted those poisoned ducks," Brian pointed out.

Molinson nodded. "You're right. That wasn't part of his usual pattern. But most of his con jobs were nickel and dime stuff compared to the money he stood to make by selling Mr. Maypenny's land to International Pine. Apparently, when his usual soft sell didn't work, his greed made him desperate enough to do something a little more dramatic."

There was silence in the office for a moment as everyone put the pieces of the puzzle together in their minds.

"I still have two questions," Trixie said. "How did David—I mean, Lawrence Howard—know about Mr. Maypenny? And where did he get the botulism toxin?"

"I can answer both of those questions." The

real David Maypenny spoke for the first time, and everyone turned to look at him.

"I'm a medical technician at a laboratory in New York City. Lawrence Howard worked there until about two months ago. I guess that's how he kept going between his little schemes.

"We were friendly for a while when he first started working there. We used to go out to dinner from time to time. He asked me a lot of questions about myself and my family, and I told him about my uncle.

"We soon drifted apart. There was something about him I didn't quite trust, and I was glad when he finally quit the lab.

"I've been on vacation for the past couple of weeks. When I got back yesterday evening, I got a call from a friend of mine at the lab, telling me someone had broken in last week and stolen some of our botulism toxin. Then, a few hours later, the sergeant called me to ask if I knew Lawrence Howard. He told me about what had happened, and I put two and two together."

"Right," Sergeant Molinson said. "Lawrence Howard confessed to the break-in at the lab as soon as I asked him about it. I guess he knows he's in enough trouble already, without being uncooperative."

"As soon as I'd finished talking to Sergeant

Molinson on the telephone, I got in my car and drove up here," David Maypenny added. "I've been wanting to get in touch with my uncle for a long, long time, but I never dared. Hearing that he'd been willing to meet me—that is, to meet Lawrence Howard posing as me—gave me the courage I needed."

Mr. Maypenny smiled at his nephew and patted him on the shoulder. Watching, Trixie felt a lump in her throat. Mr. Maypenny had found his missing nephew after all. She had a feeling that this time he wouldn't lose him.

"Oh!" Trixie exclaimed. "John Score!" She turned to the young environmentalist. "Are you still under arrest, too?"

Score shook his head. "It took some talking, but I finally made the sergeant believe that I was doing exactly what I said I was—looking for evidence against International Pine. He's agreed to let me go, if I leave Sleepyside—really leave— today."

"And you're going to?" Trixie asked.

"I am," Score replied. "I haven't found anything that the government would accept as ecological damage. I have let Mr. Maypenny know that he doesn't have to sell his land if he doesn't want to. That's about all I can do, I decided at last. The people of Sleepyside will have to make their own decision on the basis of the facts."

"No, they won't," Jim Frayne said softly.

Trixie jumped, startled. She hadn't heard him come into the office. Turning to look at him, she asked, "What are you talking about? What have you been up to? You look like the cat that swallowed the canary."

"I feel like one, too," Jim told her. "Dad just dropped me off from our meeting with the town council and the president of International Pine."

"It's good news, isn't it?" Honey guessed. "Oh, Jim, tell us about it!"

"Well, you know how upset Dad was when we got home last night," Jim began. "He woke me up early this morning and told me he'd been up all night, thinking about what had happened. He said that the poisoned ducks, along with the Bob-Whites' midnight escapade, had convinced him that the whole thing had gone too far. He would reach a solution this morning, he said.

"He called the president of International Pine and the chairman of the town council and demanded that they meet with him. He wanted to work out a compromise.

"At the meeting, he asked the president of International Pine if there was another piece of land he could use for the expansion—something closer to town, away from the preserve.

"The president said no. He told Dad that, without the profits from the timber they'd be able to clear off the parcel of land they wanted, they couldn't possibly afford to pay for land, a new building, and the equipment they needed. They'd have to build somewhere else, he said."

"That doesn't sound like good news to me," Trixie said glumly.

"Just let me finish," Jim said, trying to sound stern, although his green eyes were sparkling. "When Dad heard the president say 'new building,' he snapped his fingers and shouted, 'I've got it!' He turned to the council chairman and reminded him of that big warehouse on the edge of town. The company that had owned it went broke, and the town had repossessed it for back taxes. The town had tried to sell it, but nobody was interested."

"I know that building," Trixie said. "It's a wreck. All the windows are broken, and kids have spray painted their initials all over it."

"That's the building, all right," Jim said. "It isn't a wreck, though. It's sound inside. The broken windows can be fixed, and the spray paint can be removed.

"Within ten minutes, the president of International Pine had made an offer for it, and the chairman of the council had accepted. The offer is only a third of what a new building would cost, which more than makes up for not having the timber to use."

"Yippee!" Trixie shouted. "International Pine will expand, Sleepyside will have jobs, and the preserve won't have to be touched!"

"That's it, in a nutshell," Jim concluded.

"Isn't it all just perfectly perfect?" Honey asked.

"Not quite," Brian said. "You and Trixie have a request to make, remember?"

Trixie groaned and Honey looked at Brian beseechingly, but he just looked back at her, unmoved.

"Well, what is it?" Sergeant Molinson asked. "I do owe you a favor for helping me catch Lawrence Howard, although I wish you'd have just told me about him rather than trying to do it yourself."

Trixie and Honey looked at one another, each waiting for the other to speak.

Finally Honey said, "Well, Sergeant Molinson, what we need is— I mean, you did ask us to be here this morning, and it is Monday, and that is a school day, and— Well, would you write an excuse to our principal so we can go to school?"

Sergeant Molinson hooted with laughter. "If it will get you kids back into school and out of mischief, I'll write you the best excuse you ever had," he said, picking up a pen.

He scribbled a note and handed it to Trixie. "There you are," he said. "If you're smart, you'll devote yourself to your schoolwork from now on and stay away from mysteries. There have been enough dead ducks around here for a while. We wouldn't want to add you to the list."

Trixie gulped. "It was a close call," she admitted. "But after all, everything worked out just fine, didn't it?"

Mart groaned, grabbed his sister by the shoulders, and pushed her toward the door. "Let's be off," he said. "Immerse yourself in the intricacies of algebra for a while; you won't have time for mysteries."

Trixie started out the door, then stopped and turned around. "There's just one more thing I want," she said, "but it will have to wait until after school."

"What is it?" Honey asked.

"I want an ice-cream cone with two scoops of ice cream—one chocolate and one vanilla," Trixie said.

Her friends looked at one another in bewilderment as Trixie, smiling to herself, walked out the door.